COMPANY
of ANGELS

Also by Lili Wilkinson and published by Catnip:

SCATTERHEART

COMPANY
of ANGELS

Lili Wilkinson

CATNIP BOOKS
Published by Catnip Publishing Ltd
14 Greville Street
London
EC1N 8SB

First published in Australia in 2009 by Black Dog Books,
15 Gertrude St Fitzroy, Vic 3065 Australia. www.bdb.com.au

This edition first published 2010

1 3 5 7 9 10 8 6 4 2

Text copyright © Lili Wilkinson 2009
The moral right of the author has been asserted.

Cover design by Ian Butterworth
Cover illustration by Peter Bailey

A CIP catalogue record for this book is available from the British Library.

ISBN 978-1-84647-104-9

Printed in Poland

www.catnippublishing.co.uk

For Richard and Philip

Europe
13th Century

N

Cologne

Saint-Michel-Sur-Meurthe

heretic village

Genoa

Paris

Troyes

Machery

Cloyes

Galicia

San Pietro

Bougie

Mediterranean Sea

Jerusalem

Alexandria

270km
167 miles

one

A boy has come to Machery.
I think he might be an Angel.

When he speaks, even the birds stop singing to listen. When he speaks, his eyes shine with a light that I know cannot come from dirt and skin. When he speaks, my head whirls round and round with strange thoughts, and my heart goes *patter patter patter*.

I first saw him two days ago. I was fetching water for Maman. The pails were heavy, but Maman tells me carrying them will help me to grow and be stronger. I am not strong, and not very tall. The other boys in Machery say I am a sparrow that will never grow to be a cock.

Maman says I must grow strong because I will never be very smart, and a man needs to be one or the other. This is why she makes me eat so much cabbage. She says it will make me strong. I hate cabbage.

When I carry the water pails, I like to pretend I am in another place. It is very hot this summer, so I was pretending that I was lying by a cool stream on a soft bed of clover. Sometimes I pretend I am a silvery fish dancing in the stream. Or a white bird flying low over the water.

I was pretending all this very hard so I closed my eyes. Machery is all brown and dusty at the moment, and it is hard to imagine you are a dancing silvery fish when your eyes are full of brown and dust.

With my eyes closed, I didn't see him at first. I only heard the *shh, shh, shh* of bare feet walking on the dusty road. With my eyes still closed, I pretended that it was the *shh, shh, shh* of branches bending over so leaves could kiss the water of the stream. I pretended that the leaves were tickling my silvery fishy skin as I danced below the surface.

As the *shh, shh, shh* came closer, I opened my eyes.

For a moment I was confused. I looked into eyes that were as blue as the stream in which I'd been swimming.

I blinked, and then the eyes were attached to a person. He was very tall and thin, with brown hair that was thick and bushy, like a sheep. He looked to be a few years older than me. Maybe fifteen?

His skin was dirty. It was hard to tell which brown bits were freckles and which bits were dirt. He had no shoes, and was dressed in rags.

And his eyes. Blue like the sky. Blue like an arrow. Blue like when someone hits you in the stomach and for a moment you can't breathe.

He smiled at me, and the arrow-blue eyes crinkled at the edges.

'Hello, friend,' he said.

I wondered how he knew he was my friend. I didn't think I'd ever had a friend before. But when he said it, I knew it was true. I knew it all the way deep down inside me, in my darkest and most secret places.

'I am Stephan.' He reached out a hand and I took it.

'I'm Gabby,' I told him. 'Gabriel.'

The boy nodded approvingly. 'Gabriel is one of the very greatest and most sacred Angels.'

I shrugged. I don't really know Angels.

The boy's lip curled in another smile. 'Your pails look heavy, Gabriel,' he said.

And they were, but I had forgotten.

'I will let you get home,' he said. 'But we will see each other again. Very soon.'

I nodded. We would. I would see my friend soon. The next day was Sunday, so no work.

I went to Mass in the morning with Maman and Papa. I have no brothers or sisters. Maman has tried to birth me a sister four times, but each time it has been no more than a wet and red thing. Papa thinks she is cursed. Maman says she cannot be cursed, because she birthed me. Papa replies that I am cursed too, because I don't remember important things and am very small and find many things hard to understand.

One of the things I find difficult to understand is Father Sebastian. He reads to us every Sunday from the Holy Book in a tongue that Maman says is called Latin. Everyone else in the church nods and purses their lips when Father Sebastian speaks in the tongue that is called Latin, but I don't understand any of it. And when I ask Maman or Papa, they get angry and tell me to hush. Once I thought that maybe they don't understand it either and are just pretending, but when I told this to Maman she said that it was a wicked thought and I must never think it again.

When Father Sebastian speaks in a tongue I do understand, it doesn't make much more sense. He uses lots of names of people that I don't know. I think they must be Saints or Angels, but it is all very confusing because there are so many of them and it is hard to remember which ones are good and which ones are not.

Most of the time Father Sebastian reads to us or speaks in a voice that is all the same and very boring. But sometimes he gets excited and bangs his fist on the wooden stand and shakes his head so his cheeks wobble from side to side. Sometimes he gets so excited that I see sweat on his forehead. Or a tear slide from the corner of his eye and wriggle down his cheek.

After Father Sebastian talks, we all sing. This is my favourite part. I don't know what any of the words mean, but I make up the meanings in my head. There is one that goes *gloria, gloria, gloria* and then some words I don't know. It is the very best song. I think that Gloria is a land where nothing is brown and dusty, and the streams are clear and full of silvery dancing fish.

When I sang the *gloria* song on Sunday, I pretended that the streams were the colour of my new friend's eyes. Blue as an arrow.

After the singing, we all line up and eat some bread and swallow some wine. Then we can go. Usually Maman and Papa want to talk to other people about boring things like rain and crops, so I go and stand in the sun.

On Sunday, though, Father Sebastian called me over to him.

'There is a boy,' he said. 'A boy who has come to Machery.'

I nodded. 'Yes, Father.'

'You have seen him?'

I nodded again.

Father Sebastian shook his head so his cheeks wobbled. 'You must not speak to him,' he said. 'He is from the Fiery Pit. His words are lies.'

I felt hot and angry inside. The boy was my friend. But I nodded again.

'Do you understand? Do not listen to him. He is a child-stealer. He will take you and sell you to the Saracen.'

'Yes, Father.'

Walking out of the church in summer is always lovely. The church is cold and dark, and stepping out is like being lifted up into the arms of the sun. It was so bright I had to close my eyes. I turned my face up to the light and let it soak in. In a few minutes I would be too hot again, but for now the hot was delicious.

I could hear him talking.

I opened my eyes.

He stood balanced on a watering trough outside the church. A small crowd was listening – Maistre Eudes the smith and his wife, Maistre Mathieu and his three pretty daughters, Maistresse Claudette and Maistresse Abrial, their heads bent close together, and Monsieur Rotrou from the big farm on the hill.

Stephan spoke in a tongue I understood. He spoke of things I had never heard of before, but he spoke of them with such strength, such lightness, that I could see them before my eyes.

He spoke of the Holy Land. Father Sebastian had talked about the Holy Land. It sounded important, but so very far away from Machery that I had never really listened.

But when Stephan spoke of it, I understood that it was the most important place in the world. A Paradise, he said. A real Paradise.

I wondered what a real Paradise would be like.

It would have streams with silvery fish, I decided. Like in the *gloria* song. But the streams would be apple-cider, bubbling and fizzing and fresh. And the trees would hang low with the sweetest fruits, all year round, so nobody had to pick and store them. Cows would milk themselves, and it would be the sweetest, creamiest milk you've ever tasted.

In the Holy Land, cabbages would have honey-cakes at their hearts, instead of more cabbage.

And then, best of all, Our Lord lives in the Holy Land.

Father Sebastian is always talking about Our Lord. Except the Our Lord that he talks about is mean. He's always watching to see if we're being wicked, and punishing us for things that we haven't done, or things that we just think about. I don't see how you can stop thinking about things, even if they are wicked. Things are just there to be thought. I can't stop that, so I don't know why I should be punished.

But Stephan's Our Lord is different. He is wise and kind.

I imagined that He is fat and jolly, like a king. He has a big black beard and laughs all the time. The only work to be done in the Holy Land is to sit at the feet of Our Lord and sing the *gloria* song to Him. He loves singing. And dancing. And honey-cakes and apple cider.

When Our Lord walks through the soft green grass of the Holy Land, sparkly jewels and sweet-smelling flowers spring from under His feet.

I wanted to go there. I wanted to go there so badly I thought I might break apart like a dandelion and go floating off into the sky.

But then Stephan's face fell, and the world came to pieces and fell down as well with a horrible thundering *crash*!

'But,' he said. 'But.'

No. No *but*. I didn't want to hear the *but*. I just wanted to hear more about the Holy Land and Our Lord and the honey-cakes and silvery dancing fish.

'The Saracen,' said Stephan.

I shuddered. Father Sebastian has spoken of the Saracen. I thought of the stories of monsters that the boys in the village try to scare each other with. I thought of red, glowing eyes and horns and snake-pointed tongues and sharp hooves. I thought of them above me, with whips in their hands and steam blowing from their noses. I thought of the smell of burning meat.

'The Saracen,' said Stephan, and I wanted to cry. 'The Saracen are in the Holy Land.'

I felt a hand around my heart, squeezing. I gasped.

'The Saracen are in the Holy Land, and the Paradise has withered away.'

The trees. The streams. The silvery fish. All gone. All burned and choked and ruined. I wanted to throw myself into the dusty dirt and cry. Who could rescue the Holy Land?

Stephan looked at me and smiled. It was like he could hear what I was thinking inside my head.

'Soldiers cannot save the Holy Land,' he said. 'Nor knights. Nor kings. Nor priests.'

Who, then? Who?

'You,' he said, still looking at me. 'You.'

Me? I was small and not very good at thinking. I couldn't fight even one Saracen.

'The only thing that can save us is the purity and innocence of children,' said Stephan. 'There is no adult in the world who is untainted by wickedness. Only children are truly pure. And when the children of Our Lord step onto the soil of the Holy Land, the Saracen will crumble into dust, and once again it will be a Paradise.'

The crowd started to make soft, angry noises.

'You can't take our children,' said Maistresse Claudette. 'You're crazy.'

Stephan looked at me. 'Will you join with me?' he asked.

Maistre Eudes's wife yelled at Stephan, her cheeks red and shiny as apples and her eyes all closed-up. Someone threw a rock at him, but Stephan didn't look away. His eyes arrowed into mine.

'Yes,' I said. 'Yes. Yes.'

two

Maman has been crying since we saw Stephan at the market. It is a whole day now. She only stops crying when she starts yelling. And the yelling is at me, so I prefer the crying, even though I am sorry that she is sad.

Papa isn't crying or yelling. His face is like a stone, and he is very quiet. I wish he was crying and yelling. The stone face and the quiet means he is very, very angry. I am sorry about that too.

It is all because of me. Because I am leaving tomorrow morning. Leaving with Stephan to go and rescue the Holy Land from the Saracen.

Maman and Papa don't want me to go. Father Sebastian doesn't want me to go. But Stephan wants me to go, and I can't say no.

The other boys in the village laughed at me when I said 'yes'. They squealed and called me 'stupid' and 'cork-brained'. I don't care. They don't understand. They would be no use in the Holy Land because they are not Pure of Heart like me and Stephan.

Stephan says that I am special. He says I am not stupid or cork-brained. He says that Our Lord has a special task for me, that I will be Instrumental. He says that I do not understand many things because my soul is close to Our Lord, not down in the dirt with the other boys.

He says that the other boys are like worms crawling around in the mud – blind and pale and wriggling in no direction. They just grope and wriggle until one day they die and turn into dirt.

I am not a blind worm. I am not wriggling in the mud. Stephan says I am like a star, or a bird, soaring and pure. He says he is not at all surprised that I don't understand what other people talk about sometimes.

Father Sebastian has come to our house to talk sense into me.

'The boy is a heretic!' he says, his cheeks wobbling.

I stare at him. I don't know what a heretic is, but I don't think Stephan is one.

'He is a child-stealer. He will take you and sell you to slave-traders. You will suffer. Your parents will suffer. You are their only child. You have a responsibility.'

He goes on and on, and I stop listening. It's like Mass, except at least he is speaking in a tongue I understand.

Father Sebastian gets up and goes over to Maman. She is snuffling and crying still. Her eyes are red and her nose is runny. I'm sorry I'm making her cry. But I won't change my mind. Father Sebastian puts his hand on Maman's shoulder and whispers into her ear. Maman looks at me and trembles, then she nods.

I sigh. Perhaps now she will stop crying and let me go.

I am wrong.

It's not easy to get to sleep. I wonder if I will ever sleep in my bed again. I wonder where I will be sleeping tomorrow night. I wonder what the beds will be like in the Holy Land. Soft and sweet, I am sure. Made from soft white feathers and clover. With a silk blanket. I have never seen silk, but Maman told me a story about a princess in a silk dress, and I imagine it is like wearing water.

I imagine marching into the Holy Land. I am standing

by Stephan's side, and there is an army of children behind us. We are dressed in white silk, pure and shimmering and fluttering.

I must fall asleep eventually, because the next thing I know there is a rag being stuffed into my mouth, and I am being carried somewhere. I kick and wriggle, but the arms around me are strong. They smell like dirt and sweat and ale, and I realise it is Papa. Maman is there too.

'Don't hurt him,' she whispers.

They take me to the cow-shed and lock the door. Father Sebastian is there, holding a bottle with a cork stopper.

I am put down onto the floor, and Papa ties a rope around my hands and feet so I cannot escape.

Maman is crying again.

Father Sebastian takes the cork stopper out of the bottle, and flicks it at me. I flinch, expecting that it will be some kind of Magic water that will burn me. But it's just water.

Father Sebastian is saying something in Latin. He looks very excited. There is sweat dripping down from his forehead into his beard.

Papa doesn't say anything, as usual. He just stands to the side and looks awkward.

Maman darts forward and kisses me.

'I'm sorry, *ma petite*,' she says. 'But this is for your

own good. You have been possessed by that devil-boy creature. We must save you.'

I try to tell her that she is wrong, but the rag in my mouth just makes everything sound like *mmm-mmm-mmm*. So I roll my eyes at her instead.

'The devil!' cries Father Sebastian. 'Stand back, Madame! The devil is coming out! Look at the boy's eyes!'

I am starting to think I might hate Father Sebastian. I wonder if I will go to the Fiery Pit for thinking that.

Maman starts to cry again. Papa makes a *harrumphing* noise and puts his hands behind his back. Father Sebastian starts to talk in Latin again.

I don't think they will listen if I try to explain. And anyway, I can't because of the rag in my mouth. I sigh and close my eyes.

'Look!' says Father Sebastian. 'The devil has left the boy. See how he goes all quiet now. Now he will be safe.'

Maman makes a strange noise that is something like a sob and something like a laugh. 'But what if the devil-boy comes back?'

'He won't,' says Father Sebastian. 'Not with the protection of Our Lord over this house.'

But I'm not in the house, I think. I'm in the cow-shed.

'But,' says Father Sebastian. 'But just to be safe, you might want to leave Gabby in here tonight. So the devil-boy can't find him.'

'In the cow-shed?' says Maman.

'Yes.'

'Tied up?'

'Tied up.'

Maman sniffs. Papa makes his *harrumph* noise again, and I hear him turn and walk out of the cow-shed, followed by Father Sebastian. Maman bends down and kisses me. Her lips are very dry, and I can feel her breath shaking, like tiny wings against a strong wind. I don't open my eyes. I don't want more Latin.

'You must stay here with us,' she whispers.

Stephan will leave without me in the morning, and I won't be able to go and fight the Saracen. I will have to stay here with the blind wriggling worm-people. I'll never be a soaring bird or a pure and shining star.

It is hot in the cow-shed. I can't breathe very well. Everything smells like cow, and the rag in my mouth is sour and gritty.

I don't know how long I lie on the floor of the cow-shed, feeling sad and angry and hot. But after what seems like the longest time that was ever spent, I hear the *shh, shh, shh* of feet, and a whisper.

The whisper says, 'Gabriel.'

The first time, I think it is just a flutter in my head. But there is a rustle nearby, and it whispers again.

'Gabriel.'

It is Stephan. He has come for me. I want to call out

and yell and say, 'I'm here! Here in the cow-shed!'

But the sour rag in my mouth stops me. So instead I say '*mmm-mmm*!' and bang my heels against the ground.

Then I listen.

There is just silence.

Has he gone? Did I dream he was here?

I hear a soft scratching, and something touches my ankle. I wriggle and look, but it's too dark. I think it is a mouse.

I hold my breath. Then, with a squeal so loud that I'm sure it must wake up everyone in Machery, the door to the cow-shed opens.

It's dark, but there is a small moon tonight, and so I can see the outline of a person. It is a boy. Stephan.

'Gabriel?' he asks.

I *mmm-mmm* at him, and he comes over and takes out the rag, and unties my hands.

'How did you know to come?' I ask.

He grins at me. 'I thought we'd run away in the night so no one would know. But you weren't in your bed, so I came looking.'

I grasp his hand and he pulls me up, and it feels like flying.

We inch past my house, where Maman and Papa are sleeping. I am sorry that they will be sad when they wake up tomorrow and find the rag and the rope in the cow-shed, but no me. Maman will cry again and it will

Lili Wilkinson

by my fault. I don't want her to cry. I like Maman best when she is smiling and calm. I think of her red cheeks and the crinkles in the corners of her eyes, and I think maybe I shouldn't go after all. But I have to go with Stephan. I just have to.

As we creep out of Machery, a light starts to whisper over the purple-black hills to the east. I turn and look at the village behind me. It is so very tiny.

'Are you sad to leave?' asks Stephan.

I think for a bit. 'I am sad for my Maman and Papa,' I say. 'I think they will miss me.'

'But are you sad for you?'

'No,' I say. 'I am not sad for me.'

Stephan looks pleased. 'That is because you are special,' he says.

I feel warm inside. I am special.

'Do you see any of the other boys from your village here?' Stephan asks.

I shake my head. I am secretly glad they are not here. It means they are not special.

'They are blind worms,' says Stephan, and again I think maybe he can listen inside my mind. 'You are a soaring bird. You are a pure and shining star.'

I sigh happily and think about being special. I think about singing the *gloria* song and the rivers in Holy Land that sparkle with apple-cider.

'What about a fish?' I ask Stephan. 'Could I be a fish? A silvery fish?'

Stephan looks at me. A strange smile dances over his lips.

'A fish?' he says.

I nod. 'A fish.'

He blows air out through his mouth with a *whoosh*. 'You are indeed favoured by Our Lord,' he says. 'Greatly favoured.'

And he uses his staff to scratch something in the dirt:

$$\alpha$$

'You see?' he says.

I look. I see a big head and a tiny flat tail.

'A fish,' I say.

Stephan nods. 'But it is more than a fish,' he says. 'It is also a symbol of writing.'

I blink. I don't know writing.

'It is Greek,' he says. 'It is *alpha*.'

I say nothing. I don't understand Stephan. I don't know writing and Greek and *alpha*. I am afraid he will think me stupid and send me back to Machery. But instead he smiles his strange smile again.

'This fish,' he says, pointing to the scratching in the dirt. 'This fish is you, Gabriel.'

It is?

'It is you, because this alpha fish has a special meaning.'

I bite my lip. What is the meaning?

Stephan reaches out and takes my hand.
'The alpha fish means: beginning.'
And we start to walk.

I am the alpha fish. I am the beginning.

three

We walk all day. Stephan doesn't say very much.
I suppose he is thinking about Our Lord and the Holy
Land. I have so many questions I want to ask him. I want
to ask him: where is the Holy Land? How do you know
which way to go? What will happen when we get there?
Have you ever met a Saracen? But I don't. I don't want
to bother him.

We reach Briis-sous-Forges in the afternoon. I have
been here three times before, helping Papa bring cows

for market day. It is big and busy with many people and lots of noise.

I remember the first time I came here. I was maybe five or six years old. Papa and I got up many hours before dawn, and led Misha over the purple–black hills towards the whispery light.

Misha was my favourite of our cows. She sang the sun up every morning, low and sad. Her eyes were wet and round and when I looked into them I saw the whole world and everything in it.

Papa did not like it when I gave the cows names. He said that they were just dumb beasts, and that Misha was not really singing in the morning. She was just asking to be milked.

I didn't say anything, but I knew Papa was wrong. Misha was an old cow, older than me. After she had her fifth calf, her milk slowed down to a trickle, and then dried up. But she still sang the sun up, every morning.

Papa said there was no point in having a cow that had no milk and bore no more calves, so we took her to Briis-sous-Forges to sell her for meat.

As we climbed over the hills in the dark, I laid my hand on Misha's warm neck, and felt all mixed up. The thought of going to Briis-sous-Forges for the first time made me feel wriggly inside. I would see a market, and some of the strange people who lived outside Machery. I knew there were many people in the world, but it was so hard to picture them inside my head. I wanted to see them doing normal things like buying and selling and walking and speaking. But then I would feel Misha move beneath my hand, and a warm blanket would be thrown over the wriggliness. Because when we got to Briis-sous-Forges, Misha would be sold and she would never sing the sun up again.

As the sun slowly turned the purple–black hills green and brown, Misha sang her last morning song. It was low and sweet and sad as always, and I felt it rumble inside her under my hand on her neck. Her eyes knew everything there was to know about the world, and I whispered in her ear that I was sorry that she was to be turned into meat.

Papa scowled. 'Stupid beast,' he said. 'Stop your moaning.' And he raised his hand to strike Misha.

'No, Papa,' I said.

Papa turned his eyes on me and his scowl deepened into thick furrows and hills across his forehead and around his mouth. The early morning shadows sank into the furrows, turning Papa's face black and frightening.

I swallowed. 'Please don't hurt her. It is her last day. Let her sing.'

And so Papa hit me instead.

As Stephan and I push through the narrow streets, with buildings crowding around and above us, I remember the way that Misha trembled, and her wet round eyes rolled and showed their whites. In some places, the streets are too narrow for a horse and cart to pass. But I always walked next to Misha, even though sometimes it meant being squashed between her warm brown flank on one side, and prickly stone on the other.

A young man wearing scribe's robes pushes Stephan and me. He's carrying a stack of parchment. His hands are covered in ink stains. I wonder if he knows how to write the alpha fish.

We pass through a market square, and I see bakers and dyers and women rolling out bolts of cloth. Nobody notices me and Stephan, which I think is strange. Can't they feel his goodness? Don't other people forget to breathe when his eyes arrow into them?

The streets open out wider. I see the gold and velvet of a noble, and I look away. I remember a sharp slap to my cheek, and the strong, sickly smell of perfume. I do not like nobles.

There was a noble passing through the market that first time with Papa and Misha. Misha was frightened by the press of people. She gave a low cry and then let her stomach go. A steaming stream of dung splashed onto the cobblestones, hot and sour. The dung splattered up onto the white stockings of a passing noble, who stopped in horror.

Papa fell to his knees in the dung and bowed his head. I looked up at the pointed nose and long, glossy hair. I saw red velvet and feathers, and a mouth curled in disgust.

'I am sorry, Monseigneur,' I said to the noble. 'Misha is very nervous. It is her last day. Please forgive her.'

Dark, thick lashes closed over narrowed eyes. The noble's lips were wet and red, like the insides of a fish.

'Insolence,' he said, breathing in as he said it in a sort of hiss. Then he raised his hand and slapped me hard across the cheek.

The slap came with a sting and a gust of perfumed air, so strong that it drowned out the sour smell of Misha's fear. Then the noble took a step forward and pushed me down into the dung. He put a slippered foot over my head and pushed my face into it, so my eyes and mouth and nose were filled with wet, hot sickness. I couldn't breathe. I thought I was going to drown in dung. Why wasn't Papa doing anything?

Finally the noble lifted his foot, and I was able to breathe again. I looked over at Papa, who was still kneeling with his head bowed. Dung dripped from my face and was matted into my hair. I looked up at the noble, who was wiping his hand with a white lace kerchief. Then he wiped the sole of the shoe and tossed the kerchief away before turning and stepping lightly away without looking back.

I do not like nobles.

The church is big and square, with a bell tower rising from one corner. Stephan waits for the bell to ring for vespers. Then he stands on the church steps.

'People of Briis-sous-Forges!' he cries, and his voice is like a bell.

Everyone ignores him. I am amazed that they can walk on by, their heads down. Can't they hear him? Don't they know about the Saracen in the Holy Land? Don't they care about Our Lord?

Then a boy stops to listen. He is a bit older than me, but not as old as Stephan. He is dirty and wearing rags and very thin. His face is hungry and sour, like a fox at the end of winter.

Stephan goes on talking. A handful of people stop to listen, but they don't seem very interested. Only the fox-boy really listens. He creeps forward, step by step, closer to Stephan.

When Stephan has finished talking, the few remaining people wander off. But the fox-boy stays, crouching at Stephan's feet. I walk over to Stephan and ignore the fox-boy.

'It was good talking,' I told Stephan. 'These big-town people are stupid not to listen.'

Stephan shrugs. 'Someone listened,' he says, looking down at the fox-boy.

The fox-boy doesn't look up, but touches Stephan's boots with a fluttery hand. Stephan crouches down.

'What is your name?' he asks. 'Where is your family?'

The fox-boy shakes his head. 'None,' he whispers. 'No name. No fambly.'

'But everyone must have a name,' says Stephan. 'We will find you one.'

He looks up at me. 'Gabriel,' he says. 'Give our new friend a name.'

I swallow. Me? A name? I don't know if I can do names. And I don't know if I want to give this dirty creeping boy a name. A name means you own someone. I don't want to own this boy. I want him to go away. But Stephan has asked me to name him. He believes I can do it. He has given me a task.

'Well?' says Stephan. 'What do you think when you look at him?'

'I think of a fox,' I say. 'A fox-boy.'

Stephan looks at him. 'Your name is Fox-boy,' he says.

Fox-boy comes with us, tumbling along like a dry leaf in the wind. I glance back at him and screw up my face. He isn't a soaring bird or a silvery fish. He isn't.

'Is he going to follow us all day?' I ask Stephan, under my breath so Fox-boy won't hear.

'He will follow us all the way to the Holy Land,' says Stephan.

Something cold drops inside my stomach. 'Really?'

'Of course,' says Stephan. 'We need many children. We need their purity to overcome the Saracen.'

'But Fox-boy isn't pure,' I say. 'He's all dirty.'

He is the blindest, muddiest worm I have ever seen.

Stephan frowns. 'He is dirty on the outside,' he says. 'But his heart is pure. You must learn to look beyond the outside.'

I feel my cheeks getting hot. Stephan is disappointed. I have failed. He gave me the task of naming Fox-boy. He trusted me. And I couldn't see past the dirt.

I look back at Fox-boy. His nose is all snotty. He doesn't have many teeth. I squint and try to look past the dirt. It is difficult. Maybe it is me that isn't pure inside.

We go just outside Briis-sous-Forges and crawl into a barn as the colours fade. I am tired, so I lie in the straw and fall asleep straight away.

When I wake up it is dark outside, but Stephan has a candle. He is eating bread and cheese.

'Where did that come from?' I ask. I was supposed to be asking about the candle, but my stomach growled and it ended up being about the bread and cheese.

Stephan smiles his secret smile. 'We are blessed by Our Lord,' he says. 'Things come to us as we need them.'

He hands me some bread and cheese, and I eat so fast my stomach hurts.

Fox-boy is curled up asleep near Stephan.

I rub my feet.

'We must get you some boots,' says Stephan.

Boots? I've never had boots. We must be walking a very long way.

'Is it a very long way to the Holy Land?' I ask.

'It is,' says Stephan. 'But not as long as some might think. I know a secret way.'

'A secret path?'

Stephan nods. 'But it is no path on land,' he says.

'Are we going in a boat?' Some of the boys in Machery have a wooden boat that they take on the river. I would like to go on it, but they don't let me. I like the idea of slipping down the river in a boat like a fish.

Stephan shakes his head and smiles. Sometimes he smiles this special smile, like he knows a secret that makes him all golden inside. This is one of those times. When he smiles the golden smile, I can't help but smile with him, and the warm golden feeling fills me up.

'So how?' I wonder if we will fly. Can Stephan make us fly? I am sure he can, but I don't know if I want to. I think I might get frightened.

Stephan bites his lip and raises his eyebrows. 'We're going to walk over the ocean.'

I've never seen the ocean, but I know it's water that goes on forever. I know that you can't walk on it.

Fox-boy twitches like a dog.

'There is an old story,' says Stephan, 'about a man who was running away from a king who wanted to kill him and all his family.'

'Why?'

Stephan shrugs. 'It doesn't matter. The important part is – when they got to the ocean and they couldn't run any more, the man asked Our Lord for help and the waters parted before them, and they walked across the bottom of the ocean.'

'The ocean parted?' I ask.

'The ocean parted.'

'How?'

A slight crinkle appears over Stephan's forehead. 'That is a Secret thing, and you cannot know it.'

I swallow. Stephan reaches out and touches my hand. 'I'm going to do it, Gabriel,' he says. 'We shall walk over the mountains to a city called Genoa, and there I will part the ocean, so we can reach the Holy Land.'

My heart starts to *patter patter patter*. I look at Stephan's face and wonder if he is joking, but he is smiling his secret golden smile. I want to ask him, how? How can you part the ocean? Has Our Lord told you how?

But I don't ask him any of those things. Because I want him to know that I believe him. I do.

four

The next town is Limours-en-Hurepoix. It is bigger than Machery and Briis-sous-Forges put together.

The church is bigger. The bell tower is taller. There are more people. There are horses and carts and even some covered litters.

I am scared of the horses.

We walk down a long, wide street with shops on either side. In one shop I can see a blacksmith hammering away at iron that is red at one end. The blacksmith pauses and wipes away sweat and looks out at me and winks. It is a lady blacksmith. I am quite surprised, because I didn't think ladies were allowed to be blacksmiths. But this lady blacksmith is very large and looks strong, so maybe nobody was brave enough to tell her.

We stop near a cart selling apples. Stephan talks to the apple-man, but doesn't buy anything. Fox-boy looks sadly at the apples, and I am hungry too. I'm not sure what Stephan's talking about, but he keeps looking across the road at a cobbler's shop.

A man comes out pushing a barrow full of boots.

Stephan nods to the apple man, then Fox-boy and I follow him across the road and into the cobbler's shop.

There is nobody inside.

Different coloured hides are piled onto shelves. There are also strange metal tools and a few pairs of boots. Most of them are brown, but some are red or black, and there are even two pairs that are white.

In the middle of the room there is a heavy table with some tools and scraps of leather on it.

It smells good in here. Rich and oily.

Stephan looks over the shelves. Then he looks down at my feet. Then back at the shelves.

'These ones,' he says, reaching out and taking a pair. He hands them to me. They are brown and sturdy and solid. Boots. My boots. I have never had a pair of boots before. I sit down and pull them onto my feet.

My boots are made from leather that smells like hard

work. They reach up past my ankles and are maybe
a little big. But there are leather thongs that I can pull to
make them tight around my ankles.

Stephan pulls down a pair for Fox-boy. They are not
as nice as mine, and I am secretly glad. Fox-boy snuffles
and touches them with his whispering hands.

'Right,' says Stephan. 'Time to go.'

I stand up. My feet feel strange in the boots.

Stephan walks towards the door, and I laugh and
he stops.

'You forgot to pay,' I tell him.

Stephan seems to frown and smile at the same time.
Then he shakes his head. 'No,' he says. 'We don't have to
pay. We are the Children of Our Lord. We are entitled.'

'But isn't it stealing?' I ask.

Stephan looks towards the door, and I wonder if he is
afraid that the shopkeeper will come back.

'It's not stealing,' he says. 'We are the Children. We
are going to the Holy Land to destroy the Saracen. Our
Lord is providing the things we need.'

His voice is so firm that I know he must be right.

Stephan waits for the vespers bells again then climbs the
steps of the church and starts to speak. This time people
listen. Stephan's eyes are like shining blue arrows and he
seems so full of truth that I think I might break open.

When he asks 'Will you join with me?' I want to dance

and shout and press my heart up to the skies. But I am quiet, and watch the people. Fox-boy trembles next to me and mutters something under his breath.

Two boys step out of the crowd, wearing neat hose and tunics. They are town-boys, not rough farm-boys. They have soft brown boots and clean hands. They look up at Stephan with open mouths and nod.

A boy who is younger than me steps out also. He has fair hair that is wispy like a cobweb. Surely he is too young to walk to the Holy Land.

These boys join us.

We walk on over hills that turn from green to grey to black to purple as the days roll on.

We visit Gometz-la-Ville, and Bures-sur-Yvette, and Orsay, and Sceaux. And I look over my shoulder and see fifteen boys. Fifteen! They look at Stephan with wide eyes and open mouths. They follow him like puppies. Not me. I walk at Stephan's side. I am the alpha fish. They are following us.

I am not sure that the boots were a good idea.

five

My feet hurt so much I don't think I will ever walk again. They are covered in sores. The leather of the boots bites into my feet, making shiny raised bubbles that burst and weep clear and then turn red and angry and bleeding. I hate boots.

I have stopped wearing them, but I can't leave them behind because they were a gift from Our Lord. So I tie the thongs together, and wear them around my neck. They are heavy.

It is hot out in the sun. We walk all day, stopping in

towns and villages to collect more boys. Our faces and necks grow pink from the sun, and our lips are dry. There is not much water.

But I don't mind. I am the alpha fish, and I need to show the other boys that we are doing a Great Thing.

Some of the boys are town-boys or farm-boys. But most of them are nowhere-boys, like Fox-boy. They are sickly or lame or have faces that look squashed. One boy is blind and feels his way with a stick. Some wear rags and their eyes go wide when Stephan talks about the Holy Land, or when I tell them about the honey-cake cabbages. These boys have no Mamans or Papas to run away from. They lived in ditches and under eaves until they joined us. They ate dead rats and stole pies from windowsills. They follow Stephan because they have never known anyone to promise them anything other than a beating. And Stephan promises everything. Everything that is good and beautiful. We will all have everything when we reach the Holy Land.

We camp by the side of the road or in fields. We gather firewood and pile it high, and a boy who has a tinderbox starts the fire. It is very warm, even at night, and we don't really need the fire, but it makes us feel safe and happy. There are a lot of us now. More than I can count.

Once we are settled, we share out our food. We take food from the towns and villages. The first few times

I feel bad. But Stephan says we are Entitled, and that Our Lord wants us to take the food.

We all go forward and put what we have down in front of Stephan. Fox-boy trots up and lays down four smooth, speckled eggs.

'Heggs,' he says, proudly. 'Finded heggs.'

Fox-boy is very good at sneaking into hen-houses and taking eggs. He does it so softly that even the chickens don't notice.

Stephan takes the very best of the food, and we share out the rest. Sometimes there is not enough for everyone. Most nights we go to sleep hungry.

David and Luc, two rough town-boys from Sceaux, don't like the way Stephan takes the best food.

'Why should he get his pick of it all?' says Luc. 'He eats like a king, and we have to fight over the scraps.'

I want to hit him in the mouth.

'He eats like a king because he is a king,' I say in a hissing, angry voice. 'He is our King. He needs to be strong to lead us and to speak with Our Lord and to do Magic.'

I look over at Stephan and see that he is looking back at me with a smile on his face. He is happy with my words. I want to burst with pride.

'Magic?' says David. 'There is no such thing.'

I stand right up close to him. He is more than a head taller than me, but I am not afraid of him. I can feel

Fox-boy by my side, bristling all over and making a low growling noise at the back of his throat.

'Stephan can do Magic,' I say. 'He can talk to animals and to Our Lord. And he can make the ocean part.'

'The ocean part?' says Luc, and I bite my lip. Maybe I wasn't supposed to tell anyone about the ocean. Was it a secret?

Luc looks over at Stephan. 'I'll believe it when it happens,' he says gruffly and shuffles away.

David gives me a glowery look.

'If you don't believe it,' I tell him. 'Then maybe you should go home.'

'We can't go home.'

'Why not?'

David kicks at the dirt. 'Our Papa died last year, and Maman took another husband. He says he can't afford to keep us.'

He turns and follows Luc. Their pockets are bulging, and I think they must be saving some of the food they take for themselves. Fox-boy watches them go through narrowed eyes.

I think about my Papa, and how I would feel if he died and my Maman took another man, and I decide that I won't hit Luc in the mouth after all.

After we have eaten, we gather together and listen to Stephan tell us about the Holy Land, and Our Lord. I get to sit next to Stephan. Fox-boy curls at his feet, scratching, and all the other boys sit in front of us, listening with open mouths. There are more than fifty of them now. I think.

Stephan tells us about the journey ahead, and the rewards we will get when we finally reach the Holy Land. He tells us about cool rivers and honey-cakes and music and flowers. He tells us that we'll be happy there. That our families will be there. That people who have died will be there.

I wonder if Misha will be there, singing the sun up. I hope so.

'What if we fail?' asks the tiny boy with wispy cobweb hair. His name is Ami. He has his arms wrapped around his bent knees, bundled up as small as he can go.

Stephan smiles his secret smile. 'We won't fail.'

Ami swallows and flutters his hands over his knees. 'But what if?' he says.

Stephan stares into the fire for a long moment. What can he see in there? I look too, but only see hot and flame and wood turning black as the dirt under my fingernails.

'They will come here too,' murmurs Stephan.

We all freeze.

Stephan keeps staring into the fire. 'The Saracen will not stop with the Holy Land,' he says. 'They will cross oceans and mountains until we are all destroyed. They will enter your villages, your homes. They will burn every house to the ground. They will feast on the corpses of your parents, your sisters. They will dry up your rivers and turn your fields to dust.'

I remember my house, my bed. I think of the fire that smokes sometimes. I think of that smoke filling the whole house with darkness. I think of bones piled in cracked brown riverbeds, white and dry as the hottest part of a fire. I think of Maman and Papa, and my stomach fills with ice.

Ami is trembling, and his eyes are wet. Fox-boy whimpers and squeezes his eyes shut.

Stephan lifts his head, and looks around at us. A smile breaks over his face and he lays his hand on Fox-boy's head.

'Do not fear,' he says. 'Look up. Look up.'

We look up. At first all I can see is blackness and floating orange sparks and smoke.

'What do you see?' asks Stephan. 'Tell me.'

'Stars,' whispers Fox-boy.

'Yes,' says Stephan. 'Yes. The stars are chinks of the Holy Land shining through, like lights under a door.'

I look up at the tiny pricks of white in the sky and think that the Holy Land must be very bright.

'Are we going up there?' asks Ami. 'I thought the Holy Land was on the other side of the ocean.'

'It is,' says Stephan. 'It is in both places. It is one of the greatest and most powerful Magics.'

After two weeks of walking, Stephan tells me that

there are a hundred boys. A hundred! I didn't think there could be a hundred people in the world. Stephan laughs at me, and runs a hand through my hair.

'You just wait,' he says. 'Just wait until we get to Paris.'

six

I think Paris is the biggest city in the world. It goes on forever, houses and towers and streets. And the people! There are more people than I thought were in the whole of everything. They shove and yell through the narrow streets, pushing wagons and leading donkeys. Women wear bright dresses and pile their hair on their heads or under caps shaped like hearts or butterflies. Their skin is white as white, not brown and pink like mine. Their lips and cheeks are red. They look like Angels.

Stalls by the side of the road sell strange fruits and red and gold cloth and trinkets. Everywhere I hear the clink of coins and see the flash of gold.

Everyone stops to look at us as we pass by. They whisper and point. Some people look angry and yell things, but others clap and cheer. We are famous.

The pressing of all the people makes me itchy and my chest feels all squeezed. I gulp air and look up at the sky, but there doesn't seem to be very much sky. It's all crowded in by buildings.

I stick close to Stephan. Fox-boy sticks close to me. I don't know when he decided that we were friends. We are not. But I suppose he is better than David and Luc. Fox-boy believes in Stephan's Magic. He doesn't ask difficult questions.

'Where are we going?' I ask Stephan. 'To the church?'

He shakes his head. 'No,' he says. 'We're going to see the King.'

The King? The King of France? I don't know what to say. Are we so important that the King will see us? Listen to us? Will he listen to Stephan talk about the Holy Land? Will he let Stephan kiss his hand? Surely the King is too important to see a group of boys. He has important Kingly things to do.

Then I remember what I said to David and Luc about Stephan being a King.

'Will he see us?' I ask at last.

'Of course,' says Stephan. 'They call him *Dieudonné* –
the God-given. He has been to the Holy Land and fought
the Saracen. He will listen to us, and give us his blessing
and provisions and a golden litter for me to ride on. He
will give us horses and uniforms, and a red Standard
with a flaming golden sun on it.'

He looks back at me and smiles. 'You,' he says. 'You
will be the one to carry the Standard.'

I imagine myself marching at the front of an army
of boys, holding the red and gold Standard. Suddenly
I don't mind the crowds any more. I don't mind that
there isn't much sky. I am going to carry the red Standard
with the flaming golden sun. Me.

Everything is noisy and busy and there is a very bad
smell. I'm not sure I like cities.

Some of the people follow us. Boys dart forward and
ask us questions, their eyes wide and shining. Girls hide
behind their mother's skirts and bite their lips. Young
men scowl, and old men make the Holy Sign.

We push and wriggle through the crowds until we
reach the river. It is wide and brown, and we cross over
a bridge with lots of rumbling carts and shuffling people.

I look down into the water and wish I was down
there, being a silvery fish. Although with water that dirty,
I wouldn't stay silvery for long.

On the other side of the river there are tall, stone

walls, and a stone walkway over more water that leads to a heavy gate with a little door in it. There are guards with spears standing before the gate, and I can see more clustered on the walls and on the towers. This must be the Palace. It is brown and solid-looking.

A crowd has gathered on the other side of the bridge. We walk onto the stone walkway, and one of the guards steps forward to talk to us.

'I have a letter for the King,' says Stephan in his most grand voice.

The guard looks bored. 'Hand it over, then. I'll make sure he gets it.'

The way the guard says 'make sure' makes me think that he isn't really listening.

'You don't understand,' says Stephan. 'This is no ordinary letter.'

The guard sighs.

'It is from Our Lord.'

We all open our mouths and gasp. Stephan has a letter from Our Lord, for the King. The guard does not open his mouth and gasp. He makes a growling noise at the back of his throat.

'Bugger off, you little maggots,' he says, and pushes his spear towards us.

Stephan stands very still. 'Perhaps I could speak to someone else,' he says. 'A priest or chaplain.'

'No,' says the guard.

My heart sinks down into my stomach like a stone. The King will never get his letter. We will fail.

People in the crowd on the other side of the bridge turn and talk to each other. They cannot hear what the guard has said, but they must know anyway, from the way he is shaking his head. Some of them look worried or angry. Others just laugh and walk away.

Two men in brown robes stare at Stephan. One of them leans over to whisper something to the other, who bows his head. Then they just stand there and watch us.

Stephan shrugs and smiles at the guard. 'Then we will wait,' he says, and sits down, cross-legged on the stone bridge. We all hesitate, then we sit down too.

'Look, boy,' says the guard. 'You can't do that. You have to leave.'

'Then let us speak to a chaplain,' says Stephan.

The guard's face goes dark and his eyebrows run together. He turns and marches back to the gate, opens it, and speaks to somebody on the other side. Then he shuts the gate again, puts up his spear and ignores us.

So we wait. We wait as the sun wanders across the sky and slips down below the buildings behind us. It is nice and cool once the sun has gone, but as the light grows murky, insects from the moat rise up and start to eat us. The crowd of watchers have all gone, even the men in brown robes. But some of the boys have joined us, sitting on the stones and whispering to each other.

'I'm hungry,' says Ami. Some of the other boys tell him to shush. We didn't collect any food today. We're all hungry. But Stephan doesn't say anything. He faces the gate and waits.

Even though a few hours ago it was very hot and all I could think about was getting cool, I'm starting to feel a bit of a chill. And the stones underneath me are very uncomfortable, no matter how much I wriggle. There are good food smells coming from all around, garlic and meat and oil. Fox-boy sighs and lies down, resting his head on his arm.

I think I must have fallen asleep for a while, sitting up. I didn't know you could sleep sitting up. But cows can sleep standing, and I am much cleverer than a cow, so I suppose I shouldn't be surprised.

But everything goes all dreamy and strange and I watch Stephan who sits there waiting. I wonder if Our Lord is talking to him. Most of the lights in the city have gone out, and there are no more voices or songs or laughter. The food smells are gone as well.

The sky starts to grow light again, faint behind the rising turrets of the palace. I feel damp and cold and sore. And hungry. I notice that the guard at the gate is a different guard, this time with a beard. I wonder when they changed over.

In the early light, everything is grey and washed out.

The palace looks like it is made of mist, and you could wipe your hand straight through it. I catch the faintest sniff of baking bread, and my stomach growls.

Then there is a noise that, after the silence of the night, seems like the noise that the world makes when it ends. But it is only the heavy castle gate opening. A man in a grey doublet sticks his head out and looks at us, and then leans forward and mutters something to the guard. The guard nods, and the grey man disappears back inside the castle, closing the gate behind him.

A little while later the gate opens again, and a little man in a purple robe trots out. He has a hooked nose like a falcon, and very small eyes. He wears a pointy hat.

Stephan stands up gracefully, not at all stiff or sleepy.

'I am Stephan,' he says. 'Leader of the Army of Children.'

The man in purple nods – he must be some kind of priest. 'I know who you are,' he says. 'Your story has been heard all over France.'

'I have a letter for the King from Our Lord,' he says. 'I am going to lead the children to the Holy Land to destroy the Saracen.'

'You have done very well,' says the priest, in a voice like he is talking to a very young child. 'I shall deliver the letter to his Majesty.'

Stephan hesitates.

'I am sure once his Majesty receives the letter,' says

the priest, 'then he will want to speak to you.'

Stephan nods and hands over the letter.

The priest's smile turns sour, and he crumples up the letter in his fist. I cry out 'no', but before anyone can do anything, he has tossed the letter into the filthy water of the moat. It floats there, crumpled and sagging with dirty wetness. There is a rumbling of anger among us and we all scramble to our feet.

'The great armies of the west will destroy the Saracen,' says the priest. 'Not some dirty children.'

'You are wrong,' says Stephan. 'The armies will fail. They do not have the blessing of Our Lord.'

The priest goes a funny colour and his lips become thin and pale. 'Heresy!' he says, his voice full of wheezes and sharp sounds.

Stephan doesn't even blink. 'It is a shame,' he says, 'that you cannot know the greatness before you. You have my blessing anyway.' And he makes the Holy Sign.

The priest jerks away. He looks angry. Stephan turns back to us.

'Come, children,' he says. 'Let us carry on.'

He walks through us and we turn and follow him back across the bridge.

The crowd of watchers is back, bigger than ever. Men and women and children. Stephan marches through them without a word.

I feel a terrible trembling deep inside. Is this it? Is it

over? Have we failed? If the King does not support us, then surely Our Lord doesn't either.

Stephan's face doesn't tell me anything. It's not sad or angry. He just marches through the people. Some of them clap as we walk past, and make the sign of Our Lord. But most of them just laugh and point and say rude things.

Then there are three men before us, dressed in brown robes. Two are the men I saw before, and I realise they must be monks. Their brown robes seem much more Holy than the purple of the King's priest. They bow their heads before us.

Stephan stops.

'Come with us,' says one of the monks. 'The abbot of Saint Denis is eager to meet you.'

Stephan doesn't say anything, but ducks his head in a nod. The monks turn around and their robes swish around them. The bald circle on the back of the first monk's head is pink with sunburn.

seven

We follow the monks north through winding roads, until finally the tangle of streets and houses opens out into fields. The monks lead us up a dusty road. We are overtaken by men on horseback, and the occasional horse and cart. Farmers work in the fields, and cows turn their heads to watch us pass by.

Neither Stephan nor the monks speak. I want to ask Stephan where we're going.

I feel Fox-boy relax as we leave the city, and soon he is darting off to the side of the road, chasing sparrows and sniffing around in the hedgerows for blackberries.

We come down over a hill into a low, flat area that is covered with market stalls built out of wooden poles and canvas. Merchants yell and haggle in front of stalls selling wool and parchment and leather. Off to one side I can see pens containing sheep, cows and horses, with men bending over and looking at their teeth and eyes.

There are men and women with silver badges pinned to their simple grey robes. They bow their heads and make the Holy Sign when they see the monk leading us, and they whisper to each other.

A woman comes forward and kneels down in the dust before Stephan.

'Holy,' she murmurs, pressing her lips against his feet. 'Holy.'

Stephan smiles and touches her hair. The woman looks up and I can see tears rolling down her cheeks, her eyes full of happiness.

'Thank you, Lord,' she says. 'Thank you for coming to the Lendit Fair.'

One of the monks turns to us. 'Pilgrims,' he says, 'come from far away to the Lendit Fair, to honour Saint Denis.'

We leave the market behind us and go on down the road. It is still very busy, with many more grey pilgrims going both ways. A man with a lute appears in front of us and plays a tune, and some of the boys skip and dance. It is a good day.

The sun is beginning to sink as we enter a village surrounding a cluster of large, stone buildings. The biggest building is in the middle, and it looks like a square church. This is the building that we head for.

The abbey is all greyish-brown stone. A tower breaks the squareness and rises up on the left-hand side. There are three arched doorways at the front of the building, and standing on the steps in front of the largest arch is a small man with a completely bald head. He is wearing the same robes as the monk who led us here.

Stephan steps forward and sinks down on his knees before the man.

Could this really be the abbot of such a grand church? He is so small and his robes are quite simple.

The monk looks out over us children. I think we collected some more while we waited for the King, and at the Lendit Fair.

'Stephan of Cloyes?' For a tiny man, he has a big voice. It is a kind voice, but hard like smooth iron.

Stephan gets up. He is taller than the abbot. He steps backward, down the stone steps so his head is a lower than the abbot's.

'Welcome to Saint Denis,' says the abbot. 'This is the heart of France. It is where the kings of France are buried. It is where Saint Denis himself was martyred before the heathen priests.'

I look up at the tower and see that there is something

being built behind it – pointed and sloping. I can see stone creatures clutching the sides of the buildings, the edges and the gutters. They have wide, open mouths and grasping claws. I wonder why there are such terrible-looking creatures on a Holy building.

'Please, take your rest here for the night,' says the abbot. 'We will give you provisions for your journey. And I think tomorrow you will have some new arrivals. Word has spread all over France about the children who will take back the Holy Land from the Saracen. I have had messengers report that more children are flocking to Saint Denis like sheep to the shepherd.'

I stop looking at the buildings. More children! We are already nearly a hundred. This means that we're not being sent home. We're going to the Holy Land. Stephan will make the waters dry up and we will walk over the ocean to the Holy Land and destroy the Saracen. Tears slip from my eyes. This abbot is a great man indeed.

The abbot tells us that we may rest in the courtyard. There is not enough room for us to all sleep inside, but he invites Stephan to sleep in the guest rooms, and Stephan says I may come with him, and Fox-boy too.

'But what about David and Luc and Ami and the others?' I say.

Stephan smiles. 'They will be fine,' he says. 'But I must rest, for tomorrow a great miracle will happen and I must have peace tonight. You and Fox-boy may sit by me because I know you will be silent.'

I go and tell David to look after the other children. He nods very seriously, and puts his hand on little Ami's shoulder.

The abbot leads Stephan, Fox-boy and me up the steps and down a long corridor.

Inside, the abbey is all cool stone and pillars and arches. Every pillar is smooth and round, with stone flowers or faces carved at the top. I think it must have taken someone a very long time to carve them all. There is a tapestry on one wall – a garden full of flowers and a thin man with very sad eyes. I wonder what happened to make him so sad.

The corridor suddenly opens out on one side and there is a garden. It's a shock to suddenly see green everywhere after all the stone. The sun is very bright out here, so it takes me a moment to see anything.

There is a girl in the garden, pulling out weeds around a wrinkly old apricot tree. The branches of the tree are all twisted and bent and lumpy, but there is a lot of fruit hanging from the branches, so I suppose it must be healthy. The girl looks up at us. There is a smudge of dirt on her cheek.

The abbot leads us on.

Our room is high up in the tower. We have to climb many stairs to get there, round and round in a spiral.

It makes my head sore and when we get to the top, my head is still going round and round and I nearly fall over. Our room has a large, tall bed with a red bedspread and pillows embroidered with gold thread. There is a washstand with a white pitcher and a red jar that holds white roses.

I think it must be what a king's bedroom looks like.

There is a window in our room that looks out over the front of the abbey and the small villages, and the fields beyond them back to Paris. I have never been so high up before, and looking down at the ground from our window makes my insides go all strange so I step back.

Fox-boy curls up on the hearth-rug and watches Stephan with peaceful eyes. Stephan stands and looks out the window. I wonder if he is looking for the other boys that the abbot said were coming.

I don't want to look. I don't like being high up.

'Look after him, will you,' I tell Fox-boy. 'I'm going to check that David is looking after everyone.'

Fox-boy nods and looks proud to be trusted with the job of looking after Stephan.

I climb down the round and round staircase, and go back into the garden. The girl has gone.

All the monks have gone too, but I can hear chanting and singing from the chapel, so I suppose they have all gone to pray.

I would like to sing the *gloria* song again, but I don't

want to interrupt them, so I walk away from the singing and into a long stone corridor.

I take a different corridor and go down some stairs and find myself in an almost-dark room. There are a few candles burning in pointed metal stands, and they make strange shadows that dance as the air moves around me. There are statues of what look like knights, lying down on stone boxes. I suppose they are dead. They are wearing armour and have swords on their chests. I don't think it would be very comfortable lying down in all that armour. Each one has their feet resting on what I think is a dog, although it might be a lion. This is nice, because it means they won't get lonely now that they are dead.

It is very cold down here. I wonder if the dead knights are actually in the stone boxes.

I pass into another room and go up another flight of stairs. It is not as cold or dark in here, and I feel better. The room is full of statues and paintings. They all seem to be of the sad, thin man I saw in the tapestry. In each of the statues and paintings, he is only wearing a small cloth around his hips, and I can count his ribs. He must be hungry. I remember that I am hungry too.

I wonder who the man could be. A king? Or maybe the Pope? I don't really know who the Pope is, but I know he's very important, more important than a king and nearly as important as Our Lord. But surely if you were a king or a Pope you wouldn't be so sad or so hungry. Kings have lots of money to spend on food and clothes, and I'm sure Popes do too.

I stand in front of one of the paintings. The man has a gold circle behind his head. Maybe he is an Angel. But Angels aren't sad.

'Who are you?' I ask aloud, under my breath.

'That's Our Lord,' says a voice behind me.

eight

I turn around. The girl I saw in the garden is standing behind me. She's wearing a nice dress, but her face is dirty and her hair is wild and in tangles. She has three little silver badges pinned to the front of her dress, and one that is white and smooth and looks like flat bone.

'What?' I say.

'That man,' she says, pointing to the painting. 'It's Our Lord. Haven't you ever seen a picture of Him before?' I shake my head. It can't be Our Lord. Our Lord is happy and fat with a big bushy beard. He loves music and dancing and laughter. This man is thin and scared.

'It can't be Our Lord,' I say out loud.

'It is,' says the girl.

'How do you know?' I ask.

She glares at me. 'Because I've lived here nearly all my life and the monks talk about nothing else.'

The man's eyes stare at me from the painting. It's like he's asking me for something. He makes me want to cry.

'But why is he so sad?' I ask.

The girl rolls her eyes. 'You'd be sad too, if you were stuck in here every day.'

I look around the quiet, cool room. 'But it's so beautiful in here.'

'No it isn't. It's awful.'

'Why do you live here?'

She shrugs. 'My father was a pilgrim,' she says. 'Then he died.'

She touches the silver badges on her dress. 'These are from the Holy places we went to,' she says. 'This one is Maastricht, this one Boulogne-sur-Mer.' She touches the one that looks like bone. 'And this one is a scallop shell from Santiago de Compostela in Galicia.'

I look at it. I don't know what a scallop shell is, but it's very pretty. I also don't know Galicia, but I think it's a very long way away, so I try to look impressed. I wonder if it is further than the Holy Land.

'I'm going on a long journey too,' I tell her.

'Yes,' she says. 'You're with that boy who says he's going to destroy the Saracen.'

I'm not sure I like the way this girl seems to know everything. I look again at the painting of Our Lord and his sad eyes.

'I'm coming with you,' says the girl firmly.

I am pretty sure she's joking, so I don't look away from the sad-eyed man. 'Why doesn't he have any clothes?' I ask.

The girl makes an annoyed noise. 'The Holy Land. I want to come and fight the Saracen.'

I laugh. 'You can't come,' I say. 'You're a girl.'

Her face goes all crinkled and white, and I grow quite frightened of her. I think she might be going to hit me. She may be a girl, but she's a good deal taller than me, and quite a bit fatter too.

'I could squeeze you until you squealed,' she says, and I believe her. 'I'm just as good as any of you boys.'

'But you can't fight a Saracen,' I tell her.

She snorts. 'Can you?' she says. 'You're the size of a kitten!'

She's right. I can't fight a Saracen. A Saracen is as tall as two people and has smoke coming out of his nose and wicked sharp horns and feet like a horse's. A Saracen carries a whip that can slice through a man like Maman's knife slices through lard on a hot day. A Saracen could pop my head between two fingers like a grape.

It suddenly seems very cold in here.

The girl sees how frightened I am, and her face smooths out and goes pink again.

'You know something?' she says. 'I don't even really believe the Saracens are that bad. I think they're just men.'

'Stephan says . . .' My voice is all scratchy so I swallow and try again. 'Stephan says that they will fall down dead when we set foot on the soil of the Holy Land. He says it is our innocence and purity that will destroy them.'

The girl raises her eyebrows. I don't think she believes me. 'Fall down dead?' she says. 'Just because we're innocent?'

I ignore the way she's saying 'we', and nod.

'Hmm,' says the girl. 'We'll see.'

'*We* won't see anything,' I tell her. 'Because you can't come.'

She rolls her eyes again. 'Look,' she says. 'If you're right, and the Saracen will just fall down dead because children are pure, then what difference does it make if I'm a boy or a girl? Anyway, aren't girls supposed to be more pure than boys?'

This is news to me.

'Because we're so pretty and wear lovely dresses,' says the girl. 'And boys are always dirty and doing disgusting things with slugs.'

I think she looks a little bit sad when she says this.

I wonder if she'd rather be doing disgusting things with slugs. There is a lot of dirt under her fingernails.

'So I'm coming,' she says. 'And that's that.'

I'm about to reply when a monk comes in. He is thin, like he's made from twigs with skin stretched over the top. His face is so long that it makes me think of a drooping, melting candle.

'Ines!' he hisses. 'You're supposed to be in your Latin lesson.'

The girl looks pained. 'Yes, Father Marcus,' she says, then looks at me. 'I'll see you later,' she says and waggles her eyebrows.

I don't say a word as the monk practically drags her down the hallway.

The singing has stopped, and the monks are moving around the abbey again, carrying things or just walking slowly with their heads down. It's really quiet. I can just hear their sandals going *shh, shh, shh* on the stone floor, and the swish of their robes. I wonder why they never talk. It must be difficult. Sometimes when we are walking and Stephan is very quiet, I want to talk and talk to fill in all the gaps. But I think it makes him angry, so I try very hard to stay silent. It doesn't always work.

There are lots more statues of the sad man – Our Lord, I suppose – in this long corridor. It finishes at two huge wooden doors with metal swirls stamped on. One of the doors is ajar, so I push it open and go inside.

This is not like the church at Machery.

This church seems like it is flying. The walls push up and up into the sky. I can't imagine anything higher or more beautiful. The ceiling, which is so very far away, is criss-crossing and winding with flowers and symbols I don't know. I can hear the *gloria* music in my head, even though there is no one here to sing it. Something very large is inside me, trying to climb up out of my throat.

There are lots of wooden benches on either side, like our church at home. This must be where the monks come to pray and sing. I walk down the middle. There are more statues here, and tapestries and banners. I see a red Standard with a golden sun, and think of Stephan.

At the end the ceiling is all pictures of Our Lord painted in red and gold and blue. And in the middle is a huge statue of Him – bigger than life, hanging from the ceiling. His arms are stretched out like He's about to dive into a lake. I see Him diving, being surrounded by smooth water, diving deeper, wriggling into the cool darkness until He is not Our Lord any more, but a silvery fish, cutting through the water as smooth as smooth.

Maybe that's why He's sad. Because He's always just about to dive in, stuck there. He can't ever get into the water.

Behind the statue, at the very back of the church, is the most beautiful thing I have ever seen.

It is a window made of pieces of what looks like precious jewels, but I am sure must be coloured glass. The pieces make up pictures, and they are painted over with more colours. It is late afternoon, and the sun is low, right behind the windows. It pushes through them and bathes the whole church in bright colours. I walk forward so the colours fall on my face. I hold out my hand and it is mostly purple, with a bit of green and yellow at my fingertips. The window is telling a story. A man with a golden circle around his head and no shoes is being chased by some very wicked-looking men with swords. And Our Lord watches from above with His sad eyes. I don't understand the story, but it is beautiful.

I hear a door bang off to the side of the chapel, and I don't want to get in trouble so I run back out the door and down the corridor.

I turn a corner and find myself in the stone gallery surrounding the garden. Pillars line the gallery, and there are strange creatures at the top of each pillar, carved from stone. There's a dragon on one, and all sorts of monsters that I can't name. One has a bald head and sharp teeth.

I wonder who carved the monsters.

The next pillar makes me stop and suck air in very fast, because the carving is of a Saracen. I have never seen a Saracen before, but I am sure this is one. It has hooves like an ox, and a long tail like a whip. Its hair is curly, with horns twisting up like smoke. Its face is curled into a sneer. Its eyes flicker red, and I think I can hear it saying, 'Children destroy me? Just let them try'.

A sparrow flutters down into the garden and I jump. I walk away from the Saracen and into the middle of the garden to the twisty apricot tree. There are garden beds coming out from it in squares. The smallest square in the middle has four small trees, one in each corner. Yellow fruit hang from the branches, nearly as big as my head.

I go up and look at the fruit closely, but I don't know what it is.

'Quince,' says a voice. It's the girl again. I don't know how she can sneak up so quietly. Maybe she is Magic.

'Aren't you supposed to be in your lesson? I ask.

She shrugs. 'I ran away,' she said. 'The monks aren't difficult to fool.'

She looks quite proud.

'You can't eat them immediately,' says Ines, looking at the yellow fruit. 'You have to boil them with sugar. When you pick them they're white inside, but when they're cooked they go pink.'

I wish she'd go away.

'That one's lungwort,' she says, pointing to a low plant with green spotted leaves and little purple flowers. 'It's good medicine for chest-coughing.'

She points to another plant, with leaves like stars and sprays of tiny white flowers. 'Sweet woodruff,' she says.

'We use it to make May wine and to flavour jellies.'

I don't care about flowers. I don't care about this girl. Why is she talking to me?

She points again. 'Our Lady's glove,' she says.

I look at the bell-like purple flowers. 'Yes, yes,' I say. 'They're very pretty.'

'A nibble of the stem would kill you dead where you stand,' says the girl, rolling her eyes. 'They belong to the fairies. Fairies ring the flower bells when a human is coming so the rest of the fairies can hide.'

I look around to check there are no monks listening. This girl would surely be beaten if any of them heard her talking about fairies. Father Sebastian says there are no such things, only bad Magic that tempts us down to the Fiery Pit.

'You do believe in fairies, don't you?' asks the girl.

I shake my head. I really want to leave here. It was better up in the high room with the windows that made my insides wobbly.

The girl makes a strange sound that I think is supposed to show me how stupid she thinks I am.

'This is why you need me,' she says. 'Otherwise you could eat foxglove or oleander or hogweed and die.'

nine

'Gabby.'

It is Fox-boy. It is very early. I roll over.

'Go away,' I tell him. 'I'm sleeping.'

'Gabby.'

I rub my eyes and yawn.

'Gabby. Lookit.'

He is over by the window, crouching and trembling. There is something about the way he is standing, frightened and excited, that makes me wake up properly. I don't really want to go over to the window, but I do anyway.

There is an army outside.

At least, it looks like an army. There are more people than I have ever seen in the world. And they are all –

'Children,' says Stephan, sitting up in his bed. 'The children have come to join our army.'

Stephan gets up and walks over to the window. He is not at all squoozy from the height or frightened of all the people. He is calm and still, like the pond in Machery on a hot, dry day.

An army of children. Far below I can see David, Luc and Ami standing at the very front of the army, so proud they could burst.

'How many is it?' I ask. I don't have words for so many.

Stephan leans out the window and breathes deeply. 'Four, maybe five thousand,' he says, his voice low, with a secret tremble at the very back of it.

I don't know how much a thousand is, but I know it is a lot. So four or five thousand must be nearly all the children in the whole world.

They are all standing outside the abbey, waiting. Waiting for Stephan.

He looks at me and smiles his secret smile.

'Today is a great day, Gabriel,' he says. 'A great day indeed. Today is the first miracle.'

When Stephan walks out before the children on the steps of the abbey, they make a noise that is so loud

I have to clap my hands over my ears. They scream and chant and stamp and clap. Ami's face is already wet with tears, and he jumps up and down so his cobweb hair floats around his face. Stephan laughs and holds up a hand.

'Earlier this summer,' he says, in a voice that seems quiet but I'm sure can be heard by the people at the very back of the crowd. 'Earlier this summer I was tending my sheep in their fields. A beggar came to me, and told me he was a soldier returning from the Holy Land, and could I spare him some food. I gave him the crust from my bread. Then the beggar threw off his robe and a Holy light shone from his face. And I realised – it was Our Lord. He gave me a letter to give to King Philip, and told me that I would lead an army of children to destroy the Saracen.'

The crowd cheer again.

'For three days I did not believe Him,' says Stephan. 'For three days I thought He spoke the ravings of a madman.'

He clasps his hands before him and looks up to the sky.

'On the third day,' he says, 'I saw strange and beautiful things. Miracles. Ten frogs hopped out of a pond and started to journey towards the Holy Land. A swarm of a thousand butterflies headed likewise. Fish turned and swam against the current. My sheep, also, turned away from me and started to walk in the direction of Paradise. I tried to turn them back around, and beat them with my staff. Then the sheep fell down on their knees and begged me to forgive them in my own tongue.'

He pauses and looks out over us.

'And then I knew the words of Our Lord to be true. Wherever I walk miraculous things happen. When I entered the town of Manshymer, two packs of dogs were fighting each other. Blood and fur flew everywhere. The townspeople were afraid to leave their houses, such was the terrible violence. I walked to the middle of the town square, right in among the fighting dogs. And I told them to fight no more, and that they should rejoice because I was going to rescue Our Lord from the Saracen. And the dogs ceased to war, and stood up on their hind legs and danced with joy.'

The children all watch him. I know how they are feeling. I feel it every time Stephan speaks. It is joy and wonder and excitement and pride all bundled up and bouncing up and down inside. It is a beautiful feeling.

'And now,' says Stephan, 'the greatest miracle of all.' He spreads his arms wide to embrace us all. 'You,' he says. 'You have come to me. And that is a miracle.'

The children make a noise that is so loud I fear it will tear the abbey to pieces. It goes on and on as they stamp and weep and sing. It is a miracle.

'And now, children,' says Stephan once the noise has

died down. 'Now we march to the Holy Land. We must head east, and cross the Alps, and then go down into Italy where we will reach the shores of the ocean. And then,' he looks straight at me now and winks, and I am so proud I could burst. 'And then the ocean will dry up under our feet and we will walk across to the Holy Land, where the Saracen will crumble before us.'

We try to head out immediately, but it is difficult now there are so many of us, and we don't leave until after noon. The abbot gives us a donkey with a cart loaded with sacks of grain and bags of apples and strips of dried meat. I hope somebody knows how to cook, because I'm sure I don't.

I walk just behind Stephan, at his right side. Fox-boy walks behind me. As we leave the abbey there is a commotion behind us, and then I cry out because Ines, the girl from the abbey, is here.

'Stephan,' she says. She is holding what looks like a very long stick.

'What is it, friend?' asks Stephan, stopping.

Ines steps forward and holds out the long stick. It is a soldier's lance, with a long, thin cloth Standard attached at the top. It is bright red, with a golden sun embroidered in the middle, with wiggly rays coming off in all directions and dripping down the length of it.

It is the same Standard that Stephan described. The same as the one I saw in the church at the abbey.

'The King's Standard!' I say. 'You stole it!'

She gives me a black look. 'This is the Oriflamme,' she says. 'Before it was the King's Standard, it was the Standard of Saint Denis. That's why it's red, because the first one was dipped in Saint Denis's blood when the heathen priests cut off his head.' She grins at me. 'But you're right, I did steal it.'

'But won't they chase us?' I say.

Ines shakes her head. 'They won't even notice it's gone,' she says. 'They don't notice anything.'

Stephan has his secret smile on again. He holds his hand out towards me, and I remember how he said that he would have a red Standard with a golden sun, and I would carry it before the army of children. I start to tremble. I step forward and take it, and in my mind I can hear Angels singing *gloria, gloria*. I am the alpha fish. I am the Standard-bearer.

'So I can come with you?' Ines asks Stephan.

'Of course,' he replies. 'All children are welcome. Especially those who are blessed by Our Lord.'

'You think I am blessed by Our Lord?' asks Ines.

'I know you are.'

'How?'

Stephan is smiling his secret smile. 'I can see His Holy light shining around you,' he says. 'It covers you like a blanket. You are indeed pure of spirit, a soaring white bird.'

For a moment I can't breathe. I thought I was a soaring white bird! Just because I chose to be the silvery alpha fish doesn't mean I want anyone else to be the white bird.

Ines has a small frown between her eyes, and she looks like she's about to say something, but she just smiles and makes a curtsy. Stephan turns to me and nods. I step forward and take the Oriflamme. It is heavy and awkward, and the golden sun dips and trembles before I get the balance of it right and raise it high above my head, my hands wrapped tight around the smooth wooden shaft of the lance.

I look back over my shoulder at Stephan and the snaking line of children behind us, and nearly fall over, dizzy with pride and awe.

We walk on.

ten

We walk for three days, heading to the south and the east. Every day more children come running up to join us, until, when I look back over my shoulder at them, I can't see where they end.

Farmers and their wives come out to watch us pass. Some give us bread and cheese and apples, warm woollen caps and blankets, and others scowl and yell at us.

One morning, on the road near a place called Troyes, a group of boys rode up on horses. They were dressed in velvet doublets with feathers in their caps. Their horses were smooth and tall and perfect, not like the stampy, hairy ones we have in Machery to pull ploughs.

One of the boys – the tallest, with the most elegant clothes – swung off his horse and landed in the dirt before Stephan, who smiled at him. The boy smiled back, but it was a strange smile. Not unfriendly, but a smile that kept something back behind it. A plan, maybe. I didn't like him at all. The boy looked about Stephan's age; no more than fourteen. He said his name was Eustache de Gimois.

I bit my lip. He was a noble. A Lord. Why was he here? What did he want from us? I remembered the sour taste of dung and the sickly smell of perfume.

To join, he said. He wanted to join our army.

'To march in an army with a famed prophet would be a great honour,' he said, his voice smooth like honey. 'And much more interesting than staying at home.'

Stephan looked pleased to be called a famed prophet. He welcomed Eustache with warmth, and invited him and his friends to walk beside him.

Eustache motioned to the other boys, who all got down from their horses. Eustache stepped in front of me. I waited for Stephan to tell him that I was the alpha fish and the Standard-carrier, and that he must walk behind me, but Stephan said nothing. Eustache saw my face and looked at me through long, curled lashes.

'Today is very hot,' he said. 'Get your master a drink of milk.'

I wanted to tell him that I was not a servant, but I couldn't say anything. I couldn't refuse to do something for Stephan, and if he was thirsty, then he should have something to drink. Eustache was right after all, he is a famed prophet, and our leader.

'Here,' said one of the boys, 'let me hold that for you.' And he took away my Standard.

As I turned to head to our food wagon, Eustache said, 'and get me a drink while you're there.'

I walked past David and Luc, who were open-mouthed in surprise and anger.

I wanted to hit Eustache. But Stephan didn't say anything, so I went. Fox-boy whimpered and followed me.

Eustache is still here with his gang, talking to Stephan, laughing with him. Fox-boy and I now have to walk behind them. I can't quite hear what they are saying. Fox-boy growls at them, but doesn't do anything.

'Awful, aren't they?' says a voice. It's Ines.

I don't say anything. I don't want to talk to her. I don't want anyone to talk to anyone. I wish it was just me and Stephan and maybe Fox-boy if he is quiet and doesn't make bad smells at night when I'm trying to sleep.

'Why are they even here?' asks David, as he and Luc

come and join us. 'Why didn't they just stay at home and count their coins and horses?'

'To cause trouble,' says Ines, scowling.

Luc rubs his hand over his hair. 'I suppose even being a noble must get boring,' he says. 'They probably wanted to escape their lives just as much as we did.'

'I wish they'd escape somewhere else,' mutters David.

'Don't worry,' says Ines. 'I'm sure that a night or two of sleeping on the ground will scare them off.'

I look over at her. She's right. The nobles won't stay for long. They won't like our simple food and our dirty clothes. I smile and then wish I hadn't. I don't want Ines to think I agree with her.

Ines is wrong. Eustache and his friends stay. One of them has a red canvas tent that he rolls up every day and ties to the back of his horse. The others carry bed rolls and each night they sleep in the tent. They invite Stephan in too, but not me. I suppose it is better that Stephan sleeps inside. It is getting colder at night.

The nobles also have money, pockets of gold and silver that they use to buy fresh bread and meat in every village through which we pass. They always share their food with Stephan, but we have to make do with the stale bread and dry meat we get as charity, and the eggs Fox-boy steals from hen-houses.

More girls have joined us. I think it is a terrible shame,

as they will not be able to fight. But some of them are very nice to look at, so I suppose they are not all useless.

One of the girls is called Blanchefleur, and she is tiny and perfect and pale, with golden ringlets that bounce under blue ribbons. I think she might be a fairy, and remember what Ines told me about the purple bell-flowers that fairies ring when people are coming. Then I remember that I'm not supposed to believe in fairies.

Blanchefleur spends a lot of time with Stephan and the nobles. She often walks next to Eustache's horse, laughing up at him and chattering. Every now and then he leans down and wraps a finger around one of her curls and whispers something in her ear that makes her shriek and giggle. I think she must be very stupid.

I hoped now that there were some other girls, Ines would stop following me around. But she doesn't. She rolls her eyes at Blanchefleur's giggles and doesn't seem to mind at all that her hair isn't all golden ringlets and blue ribbons. Ines's hair is more like a bird's nest.

She follows me all day and sits beside me at night when we eat our bread and milk. She shows me how to wrap my feet in scraps of cloth so my boots don't rub so hard. And she asks questions all the time.

How is Stephan going to part the ocean? Will there be a wind? Or will it just dry up? What will happen to all the fish? Will they just die? And all the boats, where will they go? How does Stephan know what to do?

'Will the Saracen just fall down dead as soon as we step on to the Holy Land?'

'Maybe,' I say. I hope so. I don't want to have to fight one.

Ines chews on her bread thoughtfully. 'But how do we know when we're really there, in the Holy Land?'

Is she stupid? 'Once we've crossed the ocean,' I say.

'But if the ocean is all dried up, how will we know which bit of ground is the Holy Land, and which is more ocean bed?'

I frown. 'Well, it will look different.'

'So the beach won't count.'

I don't really know what a beach looks like. I have never seen the ocean. 'No . . . no,' I say.

'It's only when we reach real ground.'

'Yes,' I say. 'With grass and trees and things.'

Ines finishes her bread and swallows. 'But I thought all those things had died when the Saracen came.'

I am starting to feel dizzy. But she isn't finished.

'Where did the Saracen come from?' she asks.

This one I know. 'From the Fiery Pit,' I say.

'Where is that?'

I point to the ground. 'Down there,' I say.

Ines looks at the ground. 'Do you think if we dug a big enough hole we'd get there?'

She must be crazy. 'Why would you want to?' I ask.

She shrugs. 'I wouldn't,' she says. 'I was just wondering.'

Ines wonders a lot. She wonders about what the Fiery Pit is like, how the Saracen are made – are there women and children Saracen?

I get sick of saying I don't know, and it makes me feel stupid. There are so many questions. I tell her as much as I know, but then sometimes I am not sure if I am telling her something that I really know.

'Shouldn't you know the answers?' I ask her one day as we trudge through a field. 'You lived with monks.'

Ines goes quiet and looks away.

'What?' I say. 'Didn't the monks answer your questions?'

She looks down at her boots. 'They did,' she says. 'But the more answers they gave, the more questions I had.'

After a week of walking, Eustache comes to me. I am sitting on the ground eating some bread with Ines and Fox-boy and Ami.

'The weather is turning cold,' Eustache says.

I look at him. What does he want? There is a low rumbling coming from Fox-boy, a very soft and quiet growl. Ami shuffles closer to Ines.

'I don't think Stephan should be walking,' says Eustache, his face worried but his eyes laughing at me.

'You want him to ride your horse?' I say, even though

I'm pretty sure this is not what Eustache wants.

'No,' he says. 'Riding a horse is a hard-learnt skill, and is very tiring.' He pauses and narrows his eyes. 'You know,' he says. 'If this were a real army that really valued and respected their prophet-leader, he would be carried on a litter.'

'You want us to carry him?' Ines interrupts. 'Why? He has two legs. He's not an invalid.'

Eustache completely ignores her and stares at me.

'But we don't have a litter,' I stammer.

Eustache rolls his eyes. 'Well,' he says. 'If you can't manage a litter, what about that?'

He jerks his head towards the donkey and cart that we use for carrying our supplies.

'That's already being used,' says Ines, putting her hands on her hips.

'I'm sure you'll figure something out,' says Eustache to me. 'After all, you're Stephan's favourite servant.'

He turns to go back to the head of the line.

'Ooh, I could smack that smug look right off his face!' says Ines once he is gone.

'Right off his face,' mutters Fox-boy.

I just stare at the donkey and cart, trying to think how we can carry our sacks of grain.

'You're not going to do it, are you?' says Ines. 'He's being ridiculous.'

Is he? I'm not sure. Maybe I am the ridiculous one.

I frown. 'But Stephan must save his strength,' I say. 'He needs to be strong to talk to Our Lord and to make the ocean dry up.'

Ines makes an angry noise. 'He gets plenty of food and plenty of sleep,' she says. 'What else does he need?'

I think we could share the supplies out among the children. The smaller ones can take the hunks of dry meat and the pails of milk, and the larger ones can carry a bag of grain between two.

'Wait,' says Ines. 'Talk to Stephan first. Make sure this is what he wants, and not just some daft plan of Eustache's to make our lives more miserable.'

So I go to the red tent. One of the nobles stands outside like a guard.

'I want to see Stephan,' I tell him.

He nods and goes inside. I wait. I hear murmuring voices and a bark of cold laughter. I feel angry and sad and mixed-up inside. I wish Eustache had never come.

Stephan steps out. He sees me and smiles, and all the angry and sad goes away like rain disappearing into cracks in the ground.

'Gabriel,' he says. 'Where have you been? I missed you.'

He missed me. I want to fall down and throw my arms around his ankles and weep with joy. I want to tell him about Eustache and the other nobles and the sneering smiles. But what can I say? They smile at me? They don't let me walk up front? I don't want to seem puffed-up.

So I don't say any of that. Instead I ask him if he'd prefer to ride on the donkey cart instead of walking.

A look of such tenderness passes over Stephan's face. 'Dearest Gabriel,' he says. 'Always looking out for me.'

I almost tell him that it wasn't actually my idea, but I don't.

Stephan nods slowly. 'I have been growing weary these past few days,' he says. 'The burden I carry is very heavy.'

Burden? But he doesn't carry anything at all. He's the only one of us, apart from the nobles, who doesn't have to carry things.

He sees my confused look. 'My burden is a spiritual one, Gabriel,' he says, and I nod. I don't understand spiritual burdens, but I believe him. It must be very difficult being a leader and a prophet.

The flap of the tent opens, and Eustache's horrid face pokes out. I wish he was ugly.

'My Lord?' he says. 'Is everything all right?'

My Lord? Eustache calls Stephan *My Lord*? I always just called him Stephan. He isn't a Lord. But then I think about what I said about him being like a king, the King of us, and I go all red with shame. Maybe I haven't been paying him the proper respect. Maybe I should be calling Stephan *My Lord*. Maybe that's why he's in the red tent now with Eustache instead of sitting by the fire with me. Maybe he should have been in a red tent all along and I have just been bold and foolish to think that he is like the rest of us.

'Yes, Eustache,' says Stephan. 'Everything's fine.'

Eustache gives me a smile that shows nothing but blackness and ice.

I mumble something and bow awkwardly and run away. I avoid Fox-boy and Ines and go to the very edge of our camp where I am alone and can cry without anyone knowing.

eleven

Stephan rides on the cart now. Eustache and his boys have spread it with the fabric of the red tent, so it looks like a royal litter. They also have some bells, which they hang around the frame of the cart so it jangles as we march. The children pick flowers as we walk, and scatter them all over the cart. It looks very festive.

Eustache sometimes rides in the cart with Stephan, but most of the time he rides his horse beside the cart, with Blanchefleur trotting along beside him. The other nobles form a sort of triangle around the cart, with one boy, Alard, riding at the very front, carrying the Oriflamme. Every time I see it, I feel a sort of stabbing in my stomach. It should be mine. It should be me up there. If only Eustache had never come. If only I had said *no* when they pushed in front of me. If only I had always called Stephan *My Lord*.

I call him that now. But I don't get to say it out loud very often because he is usually with Eustache and Alard and the other nobles. This is right, I suppose. Stephan belongs with the nobles. He is greater and braver and wiser than all of us.

Whenever we get to the top of a hill I turn around and look back over us all. Ines has tried to teach me counting, but I cannot make my head go past twenty. But she tells me that there are nearly ten thousand children. We are like a great snake or a river, twisting and winding along the road, some of us singing and dancing as we go. Seeing them all at once makes me all wriggly inside. It makes Fox-boy wriggly on the outside, because he always does a little jumping dance when he sees them all, then races down the other side of the hill in front of the donkey cart, his matted hair flying behind him.

At night, we light hundreds of fires and huddle round them. The group around our fire is always the same – the nobles in their red tent, usually with Blanchefleur as well. And then nearby there is me, Ines and Fox-boy, and Luc and David and little wispy Ami on the other side of the fire.

Sometimes Fox-boy and I walk up a hill and look down over all the campsites, like hundreds of golden stars twinkling in the dark. Fox-boy and I turn round and round until we don't know which are the sky-stars, and which are the fire-stars, and we fall over onto our backs, laughing.

People come out of their houses when we pass through villages and cheer and weep. They give us bread and milk. They gather in huge crowds in their village squares and outside churches, and Stephan stands on his cart and speaks to them until their children come running out to join us. They pluck hairs from our donkey for good luck – which I don't think the donkey likes very much. They throw flowers and coins at us, and they call Stephan 'Saint Stephan'.

A rich tailor comes out and gives Stephan a robe of orange and red and gold thread. A noble gives him a gold ring with a large blue gem. A priest brings a heavy gold chain. Stephan looks splendid – bright and shining like an Angel.

Nobody throws rocks any more, they are proud for their children to be joining our army, and they know we will succeed.

Fox-boy is teaching Ami to steal eggs from hen-houses so we have more to go around. We gather nuts and mushrooms and late summer fruit from the woods on either side of the road. Ines says to be careful with the mushrooms, as many are poisonous. I always check with her before eating mine. Some afternoons when we stop a few of the boys go fishing in streams and rivers for minnows and fat carp. I like the taste of fish, but I don't like watching the boys slice open their bellies while they are still twitching, or seeing the loops of pink and purple and red that spill out of them, soft and wet.

As we travel east, Stephan sits on the cart, propped up by a sack of grain, and speaks to us.

He tells us about Our Lord, and the Holy Land. He tells us stories of Magic, and he promises us that when the time comes, he will show us his own Magic, the Magic that will make the water dry up so we can walk safely to the Holy Land.

Stephan talks so much that sometimes I stop listening. Sometimes the chatter of birds and the *stomp, stomp, stomp* of our feet and the squeaky wheel on the cart and the *harrumphing* of the donkey all get so loud, and all blend in together to make a sort of song. The song gets tangled in my head and goes round and round until I can't hear Stephan any more. And it keeps going round and round until I sort of fall into it, and by the time I climb out I think maybe hours have passed, and Stephan is still talking but I don't know what bits I've

Lili Wilkinson

missed and then I feel terrible because I should be listening to every word, because he is our King, and he might be telling us important things about what to do when we meet the Saracen.

Mountains start to rise up before us, blue and hazy, topped with splashes of white. They get bigger and bigger every day. One boy, Orry, who joined us in Paris, begins to cough terribly, bringing up strings of yellow bile flecked with blood. He didn't check with Ines before eating mushrooms.

Ines disappears into the woods and comes back with an armful of herbs. She makes a poultice for Orry, crushing the leaves with a wooden mortar and pestle she brought from the abbey, and then packing the brown sludge onto his chest. She brews him a brownish treacle that she makes him drink. But it doesn't seem to help. He coughs all night long, and goes very pale. Ines suggests that he ride on the donkey cart with Stephan, but Eustache forbids it.

We leave Orry in the village of Saint-Michel-sur-Meurthe, where a priest promises to look after him.

'It's going to get harder,' says Ines, as we walk towards the mountains.

I tell Ines that Our Lord will protect us.

'Will He?' asks Ines.

'Of course,' I say. 'He can do anything.'

Ines looks doubtful. 'Then why,' she says slowly, 'can't He just magically fly us over to the Holy Land? Or give us wings so we can fly over the Alps? Or flatten them out? Or stop the snow?'

I shrug. I don't know. 'Maybe it's a test,' I say. 'Maybe something important will happen in the mountains.'

Ines sighs. 'Maybe,' she says.

Our conversations always end like this, with me confused and Ines sad and thoughtful. Sometimes I think she doesn't believe in Stephan at all. She certainly doesn't like him very much.

'Why did you come,' I ask her, 'if you're not sure?'

'Because I want to be sure.'

I look over at her, and see her gently touch the silver badges on her dress.

'Do you miss your father?' I ask.

She sniffs, and shrugs. 'I was only six when he died,' she says. 'I can't remember his face.'

I think about my father and mother, and try to remember their faces. It's difficult. But I can remember how dirt got stuck in the lines on Papa's face. And how Maman's cheeks went all pink when she was happy. I suppose these things – Papa's lines, and Maman's cheeks – are my silver badges.

The nights start to grow cold, and we fight for the few blankets that have been given to us and struggle to sleep closer to the fires. One boy gets so close that his hair catches fire and makes the most terrible smell. Ines is smart and quick and tosses a pail of milk over him, but he is left with a big red mark across his forehead. Eustache yells at Ines for wasting milk.

'What was I suppose to do? Let him burn?' she asks. Eustache just shrugs.

Stephan pretends not to notice the fights. Or maybe he really doesn't notice them. I know he is thinking of much greater things than the squabbles of children. He just sits on his cart or in the red tent, staring at something that no one else can see. It's as if he's asleep all the time, but with his eyes open. The only time he seems alive is when he's telling us about Our Lord and the Saracen.

'Do you think he's all right?' asks Ines.

I follow her gaze to where Stephan sits, staring.

'Of course he is,' I say. 'He's just thinking of his Higher Purpose.'

This is something I've heard Stephan say to Eustache. The Higher Purpose. It makes me think of the soaring white bird. I know that even though Stephan looks blank on the outside, on the inside he is flying through the stars, whirling and flapping and singing with joy. I try to explain this to Ines, but I don't think she understands. We go back to staring at the fire.

'Gabby,' she says, after a while. 'Do you really think we'll get to the Holy Land?'

'Of course,' I say. 'Of course we will.'

Ines is silent, and I know she doesn't believe me.

'We will,' I tell her. 'You just have to trust Stephan.'

She smiles at me. 'I wish I was as sure as you,' she says. 'You make it look so easy.'

'It is easy. You just have to know it, deep inside.'

She sighs. 'I don't know if I can.'

'Close your eyes,' I tell her. 'Imagine you are a silvery fish, swimming in the cool water.'

'A fish?' she says, her eyes closed.

'A fish. As silver as your badges. The water is cool and clear and you just slip through it, smooth and dancing.'

She smiles. 'I'm imagining,' she says. 'I'm a fish.'

'Can you hear the rushing of the water?' I ask.

'Yes,' she says.

'And feel bubbles running over your belly?'

'Yes.'

'And your tail is going swish through the water?'

'Swish, swish.'

I take her hand and she opens her eyes.

'That's what it feels like to be sure,' I tell her. 'That's how you know it, deep inside.'

Ines looks at me for a long moment, and her eyes go all shiny and the she turns away. I think maybe she is crying.

I don't understand girls.

twelve

As we set off towards the crouching mountains in the morning, the ground starts to shake beneath us, and before long we are confronted with a troop of men on horses. I think they are knights.

There are not many of them. Maybe thirty. They wear crosses sewn on to their tunics, and their beards are matted and dirty. They have a strange wildness in their eyes, and their faces and hands are smeared with a rusty brown. I look at the banner they are carrying and realise that this is an Army of Our Lord.

Are they going to the Holy Land? Have they already been? They look like they have been fighting.

They rein in their horses when they see us, and make the Holy Sign. Stephan stands up on his cart as we approach them, and sways from side to side with the rumbling movement of the donkey.

'Another Children's Army,' says one of the knights. A huge scar, pink and shiny, splits his face from the top of his head to his chin. He wears his arm in a rough sling.

Stephan says nothing, but stares at the knights from his cart. Another Children's Army? There are more?

'What, are you shy then?' asks the knight, and there is a growl of laughter. One of the men has only one eye. He is holding a bone in one hand, and picking the last few strips of meat off it with the other.

'Not shy,' says Stephan. 'I just have nothing to say.'

The knight frowns. 'Nothing to say, *My Lord*.'

'You are no Lord of mine, coward,' says Stephan.

Ines draws her breath in sharply, and my heart begins to pound. What is Stephan doing? These are knights of Our Lord, back from the Holy Land. We should be honouring them for their bravery.

The big knight has drawn his sword with his good hand. 'What did you call me?' he says.

Stephan tosses his head. 'You knights and warriors have been boastful and honoured long enough. Your attempts to rescue Our Lord have been fruitless.

He can wait no longer. Our Lord is tired of your vain, puny efforts. We will show you what children can do!'

The one-eyed knight with the bone spits on the ground. Stephan closes his eyes and raises a hand. His lips part, and I see him breathe in.

'He is here,' he says, and opens his eyes. 'Can you see Him?'

The knight with the bone drops it on to the ground. I feel Fox-boy tense next to me, and I know he wants to run out and grab the bone.

'Can you see Our Lord?' asks Stephan again. 'Can you feel Him?'

I cannot see Him anywhere, but I can feel something. I think.

There is a sharp rattle, followed by soft thudding as a flock of doves burst free from the trees on either side of the road. They flap and whirl up over us and away into the sky, shimmering and white. A single white feather tumbles slowly down, swinging back and forth in the air and finally settling on Stephan's forehead.

We all watch for a moment in silence. Then Stephan reaches up and takes the feather between his thumb and forefinger.

'Do you question a miracle?' he says, holding the feather up. 'Do you challenge the word of Our Lord?

The big knight gets down from his horse, sword in hand, and marches over to Stephan's cart and stops.

Stephan doesn't flinch. There is a moment, a moment so long I think I might burst from holding my breath. Nobody moves at all. Even the donkey stays still. Even Fox-boy.

The moment ends with a clatter as the big knight drops his sword and falls to his knees.

'My Lord,' he murmurs. 'Forgive me.'

Stephan jerks his head in a nod and the man stands up. The other knights look uncomfortable. The horses get all fidgety.

'Let us come with you,' says the big knight. 'We can protect you from danger.'

Stephan laughs. 'We don't need your protection,' he says. 'Your failure will only taint our purity.'

I see the one-eyed man frown and go tense. But the big knight lowers his head.

'You are right,' he says. 'We have failed in the Holy Land. May Our Lord protect you so that you can do what we couldn't.'

He turns and climbs back on his horse. 'We continue to serve,' he says. 'We just passed a village of heretics –' Here some of the children make surprised noises. 'We dispatched them as Our Lord commands.'

I don't know what a heretic is, or what Our Lord wants us to do with them, but Stephan seems pleased. The knights ride on, and Eustache and his boys spit on the ground as they pass. I wait for one of the knights to turn and run Eustache through with a sword. I almost hope they will. But they don't, they just bow their heads and make the Holy Sign and ride away. As they pass, my throat closes over as the strong smell of rotting flesh hits me. I swallow hard and gulp down fresh air.

Blanchefleur darts forward and plucks the white feather from Stephan's hand. Then she bows her head over it, and produces a scrap of white cloth from a pocket. She gently wraps the feather and kisses the white bundle.

'A relic,' she says. 'From the Miracle of the White Birds.'

Stephan smiles at Blanchefleur, and I smile too.

'Did you see?' I ask Ines. 'Did you see the miracle?'

Ines smiles at me. 'I saw birds,' she said. 'I don't know if it was a miracle.'

'Of course it was!' I say. 'Couldn't you feel Our Lord?'

'Could you?'

'Yes,' I say. 'I felt Him.' I am quite sure I did.

Ines leans forward. 'What did it feel like?'

'Like . . .' I stop. How can I explain? 'Like everything,' I tell her. 'All at once. Like silvery fish and honey-cakes and soaring white birds.'

Ines says nothing. I don't think she felt it.

'What's a heretic?' I ask. I wonder if it is like a Saracen.

She looks uncomfortable. 'Cursed people,' she says.

'People who have turned away from Our Lord.'

'Why did they turn away?'

'I don't know,' she says. 'But the monks spoke of them as the very worst kind of people. They say they eat their own children and don't take wives and live like wild animals.'

After about an hour, my stomach begins to rumble. Fox-boy whines and sniffs the air. It smells like roasting meat. Ines licks her lips.

The smell grows stronger, as the road grows narrow and passes through thick stands of trees. It's quite cold out of the sun. The air grows hazy with smoke, and just when I think I might faint from hunger, the trees stop and we're in a tiny village.

There is a big fire in the village square, and that's where the delicious smells are coming from. I suppose it must be a festival day. But where are all the people?

It isn't a very nice village. The houses are really just wooden shacks, neat and well made, but very plain. There are no stone buildings, and I can't see a church, which is strange.

It's really quiet. There are no people. No talking or shouting or banging from carpenters and blacksmiths. There aren't even any animal noises. No chickens run around in the square like they do in Machery. No goats or donkeys or pigs. The only sign of any kind of living thing is a wicker basket that has been tipped over, spilling brown-skinned fish onto the ground. They have milky white eyes and are beginning to smell.

Maybe the people here fought the Holy knights. But there is no sign of a struggle. No weapons or wounded people or bodies of the slain.

There are some dark stains in the dirt though.

'Fox-boy, no!' shrieks Ines. I look over my shoulder and see that she is all blotchy and red and crying.

'What's wrong?' I ask.

She gulps and makes this strange noise that makes me think maybe she is choking. Then she turns and is sick for a very long time.

I walk over to the fire. Fox-boy is gnawing happily on a bone. It is a strange bone, too long to be a sheep's leg, and too thin to be a cow's leg. Maybe it is horse-bone. Maybe that's why Ines is so upset. I didn't think she liked horses.

I still don't know where the people are. Maybe they are hiding.

There is a shout from one of the little houses, and Alard comes out, dragging a woman behind him. She has long brown hair and a dirty face, and is wearing a torn red wool dress. Her eyes are wide and she is struggling.

'My Lord,' yells Alard. 'We found one.'

Stephan walks forward and looks at the woman. Eustache follows close behind.

'Please,' says the woman. 'Please.'

'Are you a heretic?' says Stephan.

The woman starts to gulp in air, like Ines did before she was sick. She shakes her head. 'Please.'

Stephan frowns. 'Your face tells your lie clear. You are cursed.'

'No,' says the woman. 'No. No.'

Stephan turns to Eustache and says, 'Kill her.' Then he walks away.

Eustache steps forward and there is a flash of knife. I watch as red starts to flow from the woman, only a little at first, then fast and thick. Alard screws up his face and turns his head away as the woman slips to the ground. Eustache's face doesn't change at all. He doesn't look sad or sick or even happy. Just blank nothing. There is a terrible scream. At first I think it is the woman, but she is crumpled and quiet and still. The screaming is coming from Ines.

I have never seen a person die before. I thought it would take longer. The smell of blood is very strong and sweet, and it makes a lump in my throat.

Stephan looks down at the woman, and I see that he is breathing fast. I wonder if he is frightened. I wonder if he wishes he hadn't told Eustache to kill her.

'Come on,' he says, looking up. 'Take what you can from the village.'

Ines screams all night. We take grain and blankets

from the village, and camp nearby. I lead Ines gently, my hands on her shoulders. She doesn't look at me, and just keeps screaming. After a while her voice stops working, but she doesn't stop. Her screams sound like a knife scraping on rocks. It makes my throat hurt, but I don't go away. I just sit her down near the fire and hold her hand.

I wonder what that woman did that was so terrible that Stephan thought she should die. He must know. He must be able to see into her soul and know all the terrible things she's done. I try to imagine what sort of things you have to do to make you a heretic, but I can't think of anything. All I can think of is the woman gulping air and saying *no no no*. And the flash of the knife in Eustache's hand. And Ines screaming.

Eventually she stops, but I think that is worse. She just stares at the ground, her breath all fluttery.

'Ines?' I say. 'Ines, how did your father die?'

She is silent for a long time, and I wonder if she has heard me. Then, in a voice so quiet I think I have imagined it, she says, 'Brigands.' Then she is quiet again.

I hold her hand some more until she starts to talk.

'We were travelling home from Galicia,' she says, her voice scratchy. 'They came upon us on the road, all of a sudden. My father pushed me away and told me to hide, and then tried to fight them. There were six and they all had knives. My father had only fists and courage.'

I squeeze her hand, and she looks up from the dirt and I see her eyes are very wet.

'I hid in a thorn bush. I closed my eyes, but I could hear them. Then they looked for me, but I kept very still and held my breath. Once they had gone I went back to the road. They had taken everything, all of my father's clothes. And I tried to help him. I found herbs and made a poultice. But he didn't come back. I waited with him all night, waiting for him to come back. But he didn't. And then the next morning, another group of pilgrims came and found me. I didn't want to leave my father. But I did. Because he wasn't going to come back.'

'I'm sorry,' I say, and reach out with my other hand to touch her hair.

'It wasn't your fault.'

'I'm still sorry.'

'When we got to Saint Denis I asked the monks why Our Lord had taken my father away. They told me that everything happened for a reason. I asked what the reason was, but they couldn't tell me. They said that we can't always know why Our Lord does the things He does.'

I nod. Father Sebastian says the same thing.

'But I can't think of a good reason why Our Lord would want to take my father away. And so that only leaves two answers.'

'What answers?'

Ines looks up at me, and her eyes are very dark and large. 'Either Our Lord sometimes does things for bad reasons, or . . .'

'Or what?'

Ines swallows and takes a breath like she is going to say something. Then she shakes her head. 'Nothing,' she says. 'Nothing.'

She doesn't speak again all night.

There are too many things going round and round in my head. I really want to go and ask Stephan about it all, but I can't because he's in the red tent. And I have to look after Ines. And, really, the real reason is this. After what happened today, I think I am a little frightened of Stephan.

I wake up to murmurs and whispers and shuffles. I look up. Ines is sitting still, her eyes still open and red round the edges. She has her arms wrapped around her knees, and she is looking at something at the edge of the camp. Everyone is looking.

thirteen

It's a boy.

He looks the same age as Stephan, but he is taller and thinner. His head is shaved and he is wearing a long grey coat with a red cross sewn on the front. The cross is strange – it doesn't have four points like a normal cross – instead it has three. The arms reaching out to the side are the topmost part of it.

The strange cross also sits on a wooden staff the boy holds. There is a wooden flute in his belt.

'Hello,' he says. His voice is quiet and soft, and sounds different, like the words don't quite fit in his mouth.

Stephan walks over to him, with the nobles close on his heels like a guard of honour.

'Who are you?' Stephan says, his voice loud and high. Standing next to this new boy, Stephan looks like a brightly coloured bird next to a drab sparrow. He is wearing his golden-orange robes with a heavy gold chain around his neck, and a red feathered cap on his head.

'I am Niklaus,' says the boy in his strange, careful voice. 'I lead the Children's Army of the Rhineland.'

I see a flash of anger pass over Stephan's face, and I feel it too. Another Children's Army? We are the Children's Army. Not them. How many of them are there anyway?

Stephan is thinking the same thing, because he says, 'Army? I don't see any army.' He turns back and sweeps his hand over our camp. I look back and feel puffed up with pride. We go on forever.

'There are over ten thousand of us,' says Stephan. 'We march to the ocean, where the water will part and we will walk to the Holy Land and destroy the Saracen.'

The boy nods. 'Your army is very impressive,' he says humbly. 'My own army is camped on the other side of this hill. We number twenty thousand.'

Stephan's jaw drops. I don't understand these numbers, but I know that twenty thousand is more than ten thousand. How is it possible?

'Are you sent from Our Lord?' asks Stephan. 'Did He speak to you?'

Niklaus nods. 'One night I looked up at the stars and saw a light in the shape of the Holy Sign. A voice came from the light, telling me to lead an army of children to the Holy Land. It said that we would have a peaceful victory, and that when the Saracen saw us, they would all turn and worship Our Lord.'

Stephan laughs. 'You are foolish,' he says. 'The Saracen will never surrender. They will never worship Our Lord. They are monsters sent from the Fiery Pit.'

I am glad he says this, because it means that all the things I told Ines were right. I look at her to see if she's listening. She's staring at Niklaus with puffy red eyes, and taking slow steps forward.

Niklaus puts his head on one side and considers Stephan. 'We shall see,' he says. 'When we get there.'

'We?' says Stephan. I don't think he likes Niklaus very much.

Niklaus smiles, and I think it is supposed to be friendly and welcoming, but I am not sure I trust him. 'We are united by the Higher Purpose,' he says. 'Surely it cannot be by chance that we meet here.'

Stephan has a sour face on. 'You want to travel with us?' he asks.

'I want to travel together,' says Niklaus. 'To Genoa, where the waters will part before us.'

There is a pause while they look at each other in silence. There seems to be a lot more going on than anyone is saying. Maybe Niklaus and Stephan are talking silently, with Magic. Maybe Our Lord is speaking to them.

Ines is standing right beside Stephan now, her fingers fluttering over the silver badges on her dress. Stephan looks down at her with contempt, but she is looking at Niklaus.

'No killing?' she says. 'You will save the Holy Land with no killing?'

Niklaus looks at her, a long look that makes me feel like I'm not supposed to be watching.

'No killing,' he says at last. 'There has been enough blood spilled on the blessed soil of the Holy Land. Our Lord wants the killing to stop.'

'Our Lord wants the Saracen to stop,' says Eustache, striding forward and standing behind Stephan's shoulder. 'And that will never happen until every last one is dead.'

Stephan nods.

'But what if there was a way?' asks Ines. 'A way to save the Holy Land without any killing? What if he is right?'

'What would he know?' says Blanchefleur, narrowing her eyes at Ines. 'He doesn't even look like a Holy person.'

She is right. Stephan looks much more Holy than drab-sparrow Niklaus.

Niklaus sighs. 'It is your choice,' he says. 'But true goodness is not born from blood and ashes.'

Stephan makes a *harrumphing* noise and turns away. Eustache and Blanchefleur and the other nobles follow him. Ines stays and puts out a trembling hand to touch the red cross sewn on Niklaus's breast.

'Yes,' she whispers, tears smearing down her face. 'Yes. Yes.'

He looks at her with his strange, long face. He doesn't look like a boy. His face is a boy's face, but I think his eyes must be a hundred years old. He lifts his hand, and then freezes for a moment, and I see a flash of something pass through his old-man eyes. Then he reaches out and gently wipes the tears from Ines's face.

'Come,' he says to her. 'Come and meet the Children's Army.'

Ines sniffles and takes his hand. I should probably turn away and follow Stephan. Stephan is our King after all. He speaks to Our Lord. But Ines is so very sad right now, I don't think it would be right to let her go off with this Rhineland boy with old-man eyes. Not all on her own. What if she starts screaming again?

I hesitate, but Fox-boy jostles me. 'Ines,' he says.

I look back and nod at Luc and David. They nod back. They will look after Stephan while we're gone.

So we follow them. Neither of them look back at me and Fox-boy. Maybe they don't even notice we're there.

We walk through the forest. The trees are very tall here, and all bent on an angle as we climb up the hill. I imagine that they are all sliding down the hill, very, very slowly.

We reach the top of the hill and start down the other side. The forest is thick and dark, and I shiver. What if there is no army? What if this Rhineland boy isn't who he says he is? What if this is a trap? I want to turn around and go back to Stephan, but I can't leave Ines. She doesn't say anything, but I can see her white knuckles gripping Niklaus's hand. She must be holding it very tight, but Niklaus doesn't say anything.

It's very quiet. Surely if there is an army waiting, they would be making noise. All I can hear are leaves crackling under our feet. I remember how hot and dry everything was in Machery, and I wish for a moment I was back there. But I don't really. If I were back there it would mean that I wouldn't be with Stephan any more.

Suddenly the trees stop and we are standing on the edge of a field. A field full of children. Fox-boy sits down hard, like he's been pushed back.

'Oh,' he whispers. 'Oh.'

The children at the front see us emerge, and stand. It makes a strange ripple through the crowd as they stand up. Like a current in a river, or the flap of a blanket when Maman shakes it out to air.

They are dressed in grey coats, the same as the one that Niklaus wears. All of them have a red cross sewn either over the breast or on the sleeve. They each carry a tall wooden staff. They all look the same. It makes my eyes hurt, like they are playing tricks on me, making lots of children where maybe there is only one or two. I squeeze my eyes shut and shake my head. But the children are still there when I open my eyes again. I think they must go on for ever and ever. I didn't know there could be so many children in the whole world, let alone just in the Rhineland, wherever that is.

Nobody speaks. They all look very serious. They are not like our rabble of loud and bawdy street-children. This is a real army.

Niklaus drops Ines's hand and bows his head. He mutters what I think is a prayer, but in the Rhineland tongue, which is hard and strange. Then he looks up and makes the Holy Sign.

The children make the Sign back, and, all together, speak three words in their hard tongue. I am suddenly very frightened of them, and have to remind myself what Niklaus said about not spilling any more blood.

He takes Ines's hand again, and they walk forward into the sea of grey.

Niklaus isn't like Stephan at all. He blends into the grey children in a moment, and I wouldn't have been able to see him at all if it hadn't been for Ines. In her red peasant dress she stands out like a rose in a dead and dusty garden.

The grey children all busy themselves. Some are cooking, others are setting up tents and bedrolls. I see some plucking feathers from birds, and others walking away from the camp carrying bows and arrows. They must be hunting for fresh meat. Why don't we do that?

Every child has a wooden bowl and spoon, and all the smaller ones are eating. Everyone has something to do, and they do it quietly and perfectly. I wonder if maybe they are not real people at all. Maybe they are ghosts. I think of the way we scramble and fight for the scraps after Stephan and the nobles have eaten. I think of how we steal pies and bread from villages and farm houses. I think of how we beg for a pail of milk.

I can't imagine these grey ghost children begging or stealing. And I don't see Niklaus eating anything at all. He is talking to some children who are lying on beds. They must be sick.

I remember little Orry, who we left behind in Saint-Michel-sur-Meurthe. Ines was right, it is going to get harder. There will be more coughing boys, and when we are in the Alps there won't be so many villages where they can be left.

And I realise something. I realise it as strong and as sure as I was when I first looked into Stephan's blue eyes and I knew I was the alpha fish.

'We need them,' I tell Fox-boy.

He nods. 'Yes,' he says. 'The grey ghosty chilluns.'

We need to join our army with their army. I look up at the white and black mountains that have been getting closer every day. There will be no villages up there. No pies to steal. No pails of milk. We need the grey army's bows and arrows. We need them to look after our sick children.

Fox-boy and I push into the grey children and find Ines. She grabs my arm. She isn't crying any more. Her eyes are wide.

'Do you see them, Gabby?' she says. 'The grey army? Look at them!'

'I am looking,' I tell her.

Her cheeks are pink. 'I think they can do it,' she says. 'I think they can save the Holy Land. No fighting. No killing.'

I am not so sure.

'Did you hear Niklaus?' she says, and her eyes grow even wider. 'He's – he's –' she stops and shakes her head. 'He has what Stephan is missing,' she says. 'He is a truly Holy person. Do you see how humble he is? How he heals the sick? He is the last one to eat every night. He walks with no shoes on. He is not puffed-up or vain.'

This makes my head whirl around. Ines is wrong. Stephan is not puffed-up or vain. He is a truly Holy person. Doesn't she see his arrow-blue eyes? And hear the way his voice throbs when he speaks of Our Lord?

Hasn't she seen his secret smile?

But I don't say any of this. I don't say it because Ines has pink cheeks and she isn't screaming, and I don't want her to start again. But not saying anything makes me feel like I am stabbing Stephan in the heart, and stabbing myself in the stomach.

'Gabby,' Ines is saying. 'Gabby, I have to go with him. With Niklaus and his grey army.'

'I know,' I say. 'We all do. We need them.'

fourteen

It is not easy to convince Stephan. I tell him about the hunting and the cooking. I tell him that it is not us joining the grey army. It is the grey army joining us.

'We don't need them,' he says. 'Our Lord will provide for us.'

'But what if this *is* Our Lord providing for us?' I say. 'What if Our Lord has sent the grey army to hunt for us and help us get across the mountains?'

Stephan's lips become thin and tight, and he turns away.

Eustache shoves me. 'How dare you speak to his Holiness about Our Lord,' he says. 'What do you know of Our Lord? Does He speak to you?'

I blush and stammer and a lump wriggles into my throat and I really don't want to cry in front of Stephan and Eustache.

I stand there, swallowing the lump and opening my eyes as wide as possible so the tears don't fall out.

After a moment, Stephan turns back.

'These children,' he says. 'They want to join us?'

'Yes,' I tell him. This is a lie, and it hurts me as I say it. I don't want to lie to Stephan. But I'm sure it isn't a complete lie. I'm sure the grey army will be happy to join us. After all, we all want the same thing, in the end. We are all going to rescue the Holy Land.

'And they will renounce their foolish ideas of a bloodless victory?'

I open my mouth to tell another lie, but it gets stuck on the way out, so I shut my mouth and nod instead. I know that the grey army will never change their mind about the peaceful victory, but the Holy Land is so far away . . . we don't need to have that fight yet.

Stephan picks at the gold thread on his robe. 'Very well,' he says at last. 'They may join us.'

Eustache glares at me. 'But His Holiness must travel at the front,' he tells me. 'He is still the Leader.'

'Of course,' I say. 'Of course he is still the Leader.'

I turn and go back to the Rhineland camp. I am doing the right thing, I know it. But why do I feel that I have betrayed Stephan?

At first the climbing is not so hard. It makes my legs ache every night, but after a few days that goes away. It is getting colder and colder. I huddle every night with Fox-boy, David, Luc and Ami, all together in a knot. I am jealous of the Rhineland children with their grey woollen coats. They make thick soup every night from the animals they hunt, and share it with us. We give them a few handfuls of our grain, but I know we will run out before long. Some of the grey children try to teach us how to lay traps for squirrels, but it is hard when all they can speak is their strange, hard tongue.

The Rhineland children chant as we march. I don't know what they are saying, but it sounds like they took the tramping of feet and put it into words that are beautiful and harsh and hurting and full of strong things like iron and trees and mountains and the sun. I start to like listening to their tongue.

At night, the stars are brighter than I have ever seen them, and I think we must be climbing up so close to them that soon I will be able to reach out and touch the cracks into the Holy Land.

Ines sits by me and points out the patterns that the stars make, showing me horses and dragons and lions, and, my favourite, two dancing fish. I fall asleep every night imagining that I am a star-fish, swimming up into the sky, wriggling and diving through the blackness, past the star-dragon and the star-lion, who roar and rear up. But I am too fast for them. I dart and flick past them in a flash of star-scales. Then I swim up, up, up, through the cracks and into the Holy Land, where I dance for Our Lord and He laughs and laughs and laughs and feeds me honey-cakes with his fingers.

After a week of climbing, the children start to sniffle and cough. The sickness spreads through us like fire in a dry field. We don't travel very far each day. We are all too tired and aching and cold. We build fires with all the wood we can find, and gather close.

Some nights Ines comes and huddles with us. We talk about how warm it was back at home, and how we miss the summer. But most nights she is with Niklaus. She is learning to speak the Rhineland tongue, so she can speak to the other grey children. On the days when she walks with me or sits with me by the fire, her eyes are always on him.

'He is truly Holy,' she says to me. 'He is kind and generous. He is the one to save us.'

'How do you know?' I ask.

Ines taps her chest. 'I feel it,' she says. 'In here.'

I shake my head. 'I don't know,' I say. 'He is certainly

kind and generous. And he is a good leader. But I don't know if he talks to Our Lord the way Stephan does.'

'He does.' Ines grabs my hand and stands up. 'Come with me,' she says. 'I'll show you.'

I follow her over to the campfire where Niklaus is sitting with some of the sick children. Fox-boy comes with us, a few paces behind. Niklaus has his flute out, and is playing a song that makes me think of honey and feathers and tears. We stand just outside the light from the fire and listen. The song tugs at something deep inside me, and I think that Ines is right. Niklaus must be a very Holy person, to make such a beautiful sound. Almost as Holy as Stephan.

Ines is crying quietly as she listens, and I can see it is tugging inside her too. She sees me looking, and wipes her cheeks with the back of her hand.

I hear a whimper and see Fox-boy behind us, with David, Luc and Ami. Fox-boy sniffles loudly and Ami leans his head on Fox-boy's shoulder.

'When Niklaus was travelling through the Rhineland,' she says in a low voice, 'he visited a city that was plagued with rats. He told them that he could cleanse the city, and lead all the rats away.'

'How?' I ask.

'Chased them,' says Fox-boy, grinning. 'Chased them rats.'

Ines shakes her head and smiles. 'He did it with his

flute,' she replies. 'His music is so beautiful that it can charm animals and birds.'

Fox-boy blinks. I look at Niklaus and listen to the flute and think maybe he did. Maybe he can do real Magic, like charm rats.

'The people were scared,' Ines says. 'They thought he was from the Fiery Pit, because of his Magic. They tried to catch him and burn him.'

I shiver. How could they believe that such Holy music came from the Fiery Pit? Luc, David and Ami are listening too. Ami's eyes are wide.

'What happened?' he asks in a whisper. 'Did they catch him?'

'They did not,' says Ines. 'But as he left the city, he played his flute again.'

'But the rats were already gone,' says Luc. 'Did he send them back?'

Ines shakes her head. 'No,' she says. 'This time his flute didn't call to the rats. It called to the children.'

I look around the campsite. 'The grey army,' I say.

Ines nods. 'The grey army,' she says.

On the seventh day of climbing, the donkey falls down and doesn't get up again. Stephan is very angry. He kicks the donkey and calls it a Saracen and says he hopes it has gone straight to the Fiery Pit. I can see tears in his eyes. At first I think they are tears of rage, but then I realise that he is really weeping for the poor dead donkey who bore him so far.

Eustache kicks the donkey.

I creep forward and put my hand on Stephan's sleeve.

'My Lord,' I say to him. 'Don't be sad.'

Stephan turns and looks at me. His eyes are very red. He grabs me by the shoulders and for a moment I think he is going to hit me, but instead he pulls me against him. Stephan is much taller than me, so my head presses against his chest and I can hear his heart beating, and his breath rushing in and out. I close my eyes and listen and feel his heart and his breath. It sings *gloria, gloria, gloria* and I feel shivers all over because my heart doesn't do that. My breath doesn't sing. I hope Stephan will never let go, that I can stay here forever listening to his heart singing *gloria*.

But Eustache clears his throat and Stephan steps away and I can see that the tears have left his eyes and travelled down to his cheeks. He sniffs.

'Stephan,' I say, and then blush for saying his name aloud, but I've started now and have to finish. 'Stephan, the donkey was old. It's not your fault he died.'

Stephan frowns. 'My fault?' he says.

Eustache shoves me, hard, so I fall down to my hands and knees. 'His fault? How can you say that? How could it ever be his fault? That stupid donkey was honoured to carry His Holiness. Every day that the donkey got to pull

Lili Wilkinson

that cart was another day bringing him closer to Our Lord. How dare you?'

He kicks dust into my face and my eyes sting and water, and I blink. Why doesn't Stephan stop him? Stephan, who just embraced me and cried onto the top of my head?

'You should make *him* pull the cart,' says Blanchefleur with a giggling sneer.

Eustache kicks the donkey again, and for a moment I really think he will. He'll make me pull the cart with Stephan on it up the mountain, and I will fall over one day and not get up just like the donkey.

But he doesn't. Instead he calls Alard over and tells him that Stephan will be riding his horse. Alard's face falls.

'Eustache,' he says. 'This is getting dangerous. It isn't fun any more.'

Eustache glares at him. 'So what? You're getting frightened? Do you want to crawl home to your mother's skirts?'

Alard looks like that is exactly what he wants. 'No,' he says. 'Of course not. But –'

'But nothing!'

Eustache looks different now. Maybe it is just because he is thinner, but his lazy smile and sneer are gone and his eyes have become all hard. He barely speaks to the other nobles now – every minute of his day is spent fixed on Stephan.

I want to ask why he doesn't let Stephan ride his own horse, but my mouth is still full of dirt so I don't.

So now, as we climb, Eustache goes first, bearing the Oriflamme and leading Stephan's horse behind him. They drape the horse in some of the red and gold fabric and bells that they had on the cart, and leave the cart behind.

'Why don't we cut it up and use it for firewood?' says Ines.

Eustache shoots her a look of disgust. 'Because this is the cart that bore His Holiness,' he says. 'It's sacred. A relic. Pilgrimages will be made to this place to visit the Holy Cart.'

Ines snorts, and goes to walk with Niklaus, who has been watching. I look at the cart and wonder if it really is Holy, if Stephan's goodness and his *gloria* heartbeat have soaked into it and made it something beautiful.

And then I wonder that about me. Did Stephan's *gloria* soak into me when he held me and I listened to his heart? Does that make me a beautiful and Holy thing?

fifteen

Today we see snow for the first time. It's hard to believe that it is still summer in Machery. The green hills and valleys are gone, and now everything is cold and grey.

Many of the children have no shoes, and some stay up crying because their feet hurt. I am very glad to have my boots, but I wish I could share them with the other children. I see one boy with toes that are all black and tiny, like they have been burnt. I ask him if he put his feet too close to the fire, but he shakes his head.

'Maman?' he asks, looking at me with eyes that don't really see.

He is shivering all over, so I give him my blanket, and go and share with Fox-boy.

It snows properly during the night, and nobody gets much sleep, except maybe the nobles in the red tent.

When the sun rises, everything is changed. The snow is crisp and as white as a river as it rushes around a corner, and it makes me sing inside.

Everyone is excited, and we throw snowballs and play and laugh, even the nobles.

The trees here are small and twisted, and snow lies heavily on their branches. I don't think I have ever seen anything so white. It is whiter than a noble's beard. Whiter than an Angel's teeth. Whiter than the corners of Maman's eyes. I want to be a soaring white bird flashing over the snow, so white that I can't be seen.

We have no dry firewood left, but I don't care. The mountain can't be so dangerous, not if it is so beautiful.

I go to find the shivering boy to see if his toes are better, but he isn't where I left him. He must be off playing somewhere. I smile and pick up my blanket from where it is lying, half buried under the snow. Towards the edge of the camp I can see another scrap of fabric poking out from the snow, so I go and tug it out to make sure it doesn't get lost. We barely have enough blankets as it is, without losing more.

It's not a blanket. It's a tunic, the brown woollen kind that we boys all wear. I wonder who isn't wearing his. They must be cold. There is a pair of farmer's trews here too, and a woollen cap. I collect all these things, and then, right at the edge of the camp, I see it.

A hand.

At first I don't think it is a hand, because it isn't pink at all. It's white and blue and black and purple. And if it is a hand, where is the rest of the person that it belongs to?

The hand is sticking out of a hump of snow. I reach out and touch it. It is frozen. I reach out and grab the hand and pull, and the hump of snow falls away, and the shivering boy is underneath.

He's not shivering any more.

He is naked, and his body is blue and white, except for his hands, feet and nose, which are black as iron. His eyes are open, but I know he isn't going to see anything ever again.

I try to dig the shivering boy a grave, but the ground is too hard. So I just heap snow over him, and put a stone on top of the snow to mark it. Fox-boy helps me heap the snow, down on all fours and scrabbling at the cold wet whiteness. His knees get all soaked, and wetness drips from his nose.

I want Stephan to come and say a prayer for the shivering boy, but Alard, who is guarding the red tent, says it is too cold for Stephan to come out. He says Stephan is busy talking with Our Lord, and with Eustache, deciding the best way to go.

'Gabby?' It is Ines, counting out dried leaves from a pouch into her palm. 'What's wrong?'

I try to look brave. 'A boy is dead,' I tell her. 'He was shivering but then he took off all his clothes and I found him under the snow. Bits of him went black. I have made a grave but it is too cold for Stephan to say a prayer.'

Ines reaches out and grabs my hand. 'Let's find Niklaus,' she says. 'He can say the prayer.'

Niklaus stands over the snow grave with his three-pronged cross and speaks in his strange tongue, quiet and low. His eyes are sad. He makes the Holy Sign.

'Did you know this boy?' he asks me.

'I lent him my blanket,' I say. 'But I didn't know his name.'

'Does anyone know him here? Does he have friends? Or brothers?'

I spread my hands. 'I don't know.'

Niklaus nods slowly. He must be cold with his head all shaved like that. Someone should steal him a hat.

'We must be his family, then,' says Niklaus. 'We must wish him a fast journey to the side of Our Lord.'

He closes his eyes, and I do too. I pray for the shivering boy, and ask Our Lord to help him. I wonder if we will see him again, when we reach the Holy Land.

When I open my eyes, Fox-boy is on his hands and knees, down before the snow grave. He lays his cheek against the snow. 'Bruvver,' he says. 'Fambly.'

I wonder if Fox-boy has ever had a family, before us.

The shivering boy is the first one of us to die, but he is not the last. Every night we go to sleep, and every morning there are more children who do not get up. Many of them are like the shivering boy – they tear off their clothes and bury themselves in the snow.

I ask Stephan why this is, and he looks thoughtful.

'They are wicked children,' he says at last. 'Burning with the fire of the Pit inside their hearts. That's why they want to cool off in the snow.'

I didn't think the shivering boy had been wicked.

I look at Ines, who is sitting nearby. She is listening to us talk. I wait for her to argue with Stephan. I wait for her to say, 'but I thought all children were innocent'. I wait for her to ask how he knows they were wicked, or what they did to be so wicked. But she doesn't say anything, she just turns and watches Niklaus as he helps a sick child to drink some melted snow.

So I ask him for her. 'What did they do?' I say. 'What made them so wicked?'

Stephan shrugs. 'That's not for me to say,' he said. 'But their souls are dark. That's why their fingers and toes turn black, because of the evil inside leaking out.'

'Nonsense.'

It is Niklaus, come over to us. Ines hovers behind him.

Stephan looks at him, and I see his top lip twitch. 'What did you say to me?'

Niklaus's old-man eyes are calm. 'These children are not wicked,' he says. 'They are pure and innocent, and they are freezing to death in this cold.'

'Really?' says Stephan. 'Then if they are so cold, why do they take off their clothes?'

A small frown crinkles Niklaus's forehead. 'I don't know,' he says. 'But it is surely a sign of a sickness from the cold, or perhaps from the great height. They become confused and don't know where they are. They shiver and are sick. They can no longer walk or use their hands. And then they die.'

Stephan laughs. 'He doesn't know,' he says, speaking to the rest of us. 'He says it himself. He doesn't know what's wrong with the children. Well I know. They are wicked. They deserve to die.'

'Nobody deserves to die,' says Niklaus. 'Be they child or heretic or Saracen. Nobody.'

A look of revulsion sweeps over Stephan's face.

'You are disgusting,' he says. 'You are no better than them. You are a lover or heretics and Saracens. An animal. Worse.'

For a moment there is a terrible look in Niklaus's eyes, and I think he is going to hit Stephan, even kill him. But the look is swallowed and replaced by a look of pity. Niklaus shakes his head.

'I am going to pray for the dead children,' he says. 'And do what I can for the living.'

'Suit yourself,' says Stephan. 'Waste your time.'

sixteen

It gets worse. Soon there are no trees or plants at all, just walls of rock and snow and ice. We run out of food, and have to make do with eating snow and sharing out pathetic mouthfuls of meat from rabbits and birds. There is no more wood, so no more fires. We eat our meat raw, and huddle together at night.

Every morning we leave behind more and more dead children, still sleeping in the snow. We grow too weak to even cover them over. We just walk on.

One bitter afternoon it is little Ami who stumbles in the snow and doesn't get up.

Luc and David are walking a little further ahead, so they don't notice. But Fox-boy does, and he scrambles over the snow and tries to pull Ami to his feet. But Ami won't get up. His jaw is hanging slack and his eyes are empty.

'Fox-boy,' I say. 'Leave him.'

Fox-boy looks up at me, his face sad and angry.

'No,' he says, and I can tell he is disappointed in me. He thinks that we can save Ami. He doesn't know it's too late.

Someone grabs my sleeve. It is Alard. I look around, but I can't see Eustache or any of the nobles. They don't often come back away from the front of the line.

'Your friend is dead,' he says. 'I'm sorry.'

I don't say anything. If I open my mouth, it just lets more cold in.

'Others will die,' says Alard. 'We could all die.'

He keeps glancing around, as if he is nervous of getting caught talking to me.

'It was supposed to be fun,' he says. 'An adventure. Eustache promised we'd go home once it got boring. But now people are dying, and it's not fun any more.'

'So why don't you go home?' I ask.

'I can't leave without Eustache and the others,' he says. 'It would be unchivalrous.'

I don't know that word, but I think I understand. 'Why are you telling me this?'

Alard leans his face close to mine. 'Talk to Stephan,' he says. 'He trusts you. He listens to you. Tell him to turn around.'

'But then we'll never get to the Holy Land!'

Alard sighs, and his breath turns to white clouds around my face. 'We won't get there anyway if we're all dead. We are not knights or warriors. We're just children. It's time to go home.'

As the shadows creep in and we burrow into the snow and huddle close together, I think about what Alard said.

What if he was right? What if we all die up here, on the mountain. Then everything will be wasted. What if there are not enough of us to carry Stephan's litter? What if he himself falls in the snow and dies?

I close my eyes and see the black-tipped hand of the shivering boy, poking out of the snow. I see myself grab the hand and pull it, but it is not the body of the shivering boy that emerges. It is Stephan. I let out a little cry and open my eyes. Fox-boy wriggles closer to me.

'Ami,' he whispers. 'Gone.'

I pat him on the head. Who would be next? Fox-boy? Ines? Me? I believe in Stephan. I do. But what if I am wrong?

What if believing isn't enough?

But Eustache changed. Alard says he only joined us for fun, but now he truly believes in Stephan. I can tell. And he is a noble and, although he is mean, he knows things. He can read letters and knows about numbers and Saints and Angels.

I need to talk to Stephan. I need to ask him if we are doing the right thing. I need to be sure.

But I don't want Eustache to know that Alard spoke to me, and Eustache is always near Stephan.

So I go to Niklaus.

He and Ines are tending to the youngest children, rubbing pinkness back into blue feet and hands. Ines occasionally mixes a pinch of herbs from her pouch with a handful of snow, and feeds it to some of the children. She looks up as I approach.

The evening has turned the snow blue and grey. When Ines stands up, she pauses and sways for a moment. She is very thin. I hope she is getting enough food and rest. Although none of us are, really.

'Gabriel,' says Niklaus. 'Welcome.'

I have never really spoken to him before, so I am surprised he knows my name.

'I . . .' I'm not sure what to say.

'Tell me how I can help.'

I swallow, and tell him about my talk with Alard. I tell him about Ami.

'Is this right?' I ask. 'Are we doing the right thing?'

Niklaus rubs his forehead and closes his old-man eyes. Then his shoulders straighten.

'Yes,' he says. 'I know it's hard. And more will die. I cannot save them all. But we are doing the work of Our Lord, so we must struggle on.'

'But if it is the work of Our Lord, then why doesn't He protect us?' I ask. 'Why is He letting us die?'

'I don't know,' he says. 'I don't think Our Lord can control who lives and dies.'

I feel tears burning behind my eyes. 'What good is He, then?'

Niklaus puts his hands on my shoulders. 'He gives us hope,' he says. 'And while we still live and breathe, there is hope. And every step we take in the snow is one step closer to the Holy Land. We'll get there, Gabriel. I promise.'

He promised. I look over at Ines and see her eyes shining. Ines believes him. And she is always so full of questions.

Ines believes in what we are doing. Eustache believes. And Stephan and Niklaus believe.

I must believe too.

One by one, the horses fall down in the snow and die. When this happens, we rush at the dead bodies like wild animals and strip them to the bone.

Stephan's horse is last to fall. He forbids us from eating it, as it is a Holy animal for bearing him. He is right, but I am so hungry that I don't care. Eustache orders us to fashion a litter for Stephan out of the canvas red tent, and we take it in turns to carry him up the mountain. He is so swaddled in blankets that we can barely see his face, and he mutters strange words and barks hoarse commands at us that we can't understand. Eustache has to translate.

Niklaus walks in front of all of us, his feet bare and his head uncovered. He has not shaved it again though, and his hair is growing back, a soft, pale fuzz. He doesn't seem to suffer from the cold.

The smallest children are the first to die. Especially the ones with no shoes. Their feet either go black and stop working, or are cut open on the sharp rocks under the snow. If Stephan is right, and the blackness is evil leaking out from inside them, there are many evil children in our army.

The grey army share their coats and blankets with us, but they fare no better.

We pass over huge canyons, and many children slip and plunge to their deaths. We try to stop and say a prayer for each one, but sometimes nobody notices. Others sit down to rest, and never get up again. In the end, we just pray every night for the children that leave us each day.

Every morning when we set out, I look back at the giant snake of children winding behind us, and every morning the snake is a little shorter, a little thinner. There are no fires at night any more, no blankets of golden stars. Just darkness and ice.

Ines says that there is less air up on the mountain. I think she must be right, because it is hard to breathe and my head feels light and I am a little dizzy, although that could be from being so hungry.

The children are starting to turn wild, and I hear rumours that they are eating the raw, frozen corpses of the others. But I pretend I don't hear those things. I just walk, on and on, trying to ignore the hollow, sick feeling in my belly and the dizziness in my head.

Fox-boy grows even thinner, and his twitches get bigger. Sometimes he falls down into the snow and twitches and jerks and white comes out of his mouth. I stop and put my hand on his forehead and wait with him until he stops. The attacks don't usually last very long, although I think they are getting worse.

We are so high now, I feel like we must nearly be at the very top of the world. Sometimes the snow is so deep it buries us completely. Then we have to carve out little burrows to sleep in until the snow is hard enough for us to walk on. On other days, the sky is so blue it makes my teeth ache, and the sun's reflection on the snow is so bright that we can barely see at all.

Lili Wilkinson

On these days, Stephan gets very excited and starts to cry out about glory and the Holy Land and Our Lord. I try to listen, but his words are all turned around the wrong way, and I can't understand what he's saying. But his voice throbs with such *knowing* that I feel a bit warmer.

A snowstorm starts one night, and doesn't stop. We struggle through it for what we think must be the morning, but nobody is really sure because it's so dark and whirling and cold.

We dig out burrows under a sheltered overhang of rock and huddle up together like animals in dens. Some of the children cry, others whisper prayers. But most of us just huddle and shiver. I try not to fall asleep, because I have noticed that the children who sleep are more often than not the children who don't get up again. Fox-boy curls tight around me, and I don't even notice his bad smells any more. I am grateful for his warmth.

I listen to the sound of the wind and the snow. It screeches and there are shuddering thumps as snow slides and falls. I hope none of it falls on us. I try to sing the *gloria* song, but I don't really know the words, so I just mutter the *gloria, gloria* bit over and over again.

And just like I've called him up, suddenly Stephan is there, crouching in the half-dark of the storm.

'It's time,' he says. His voice is thin and sharp.

'Time for what?' I ask, as the children around me stir and wake and look up at him.

'Time for walking,' he says. 'Time for the Army of Children to fight the Saracen. We have to go now.'

'But the storm –'

Stephan shakes his head and looks angry. 'There is no storm,' he says. 'It's an illusion, created by the Saracen to trick us.'

'No,' I say, and I can't believe that it is me saying this, that I am saying *no* to our King. 'The storm is real.'

Something is behind Stephan, stepping out of the storm. A shadow, red with blood. I feel dizzy. It's Eustache. He has the Oriflamme in his hand.

'Do you doubt His Holiness?' he says. 'If you speak against Him, you are an apostate.'

I don't know what an apostate is, but I don't think I am one. Fox-boy and Luc and David stare at me, their eyes wide.

Alard moves forward. 'I think Gabriel is right,' he says. 'We should stay until the storm passes.'

Eustache hisses at him. 'Get out,' he says, his voice low. 'I'll deal with you later.'

Alard and Eustache stare at each other for a long time, then Alard turns and disappears into the storm.

But I am not finished.

'It's too dangerous,' I say. 'Enough of us have died already. If we go out now, we will all die.'

I feel a great shock across the side of my head, and suddenly I am lying in the snow, my ear all hot and beating. Eustache stands above me, holding the Oriflamme high. I hear the other children murmuring to each other, and Blanchefleur's high giggle.

'Apostate,' Eustache hisses, and brings the Oriflamme down on me again. The wood cracks against my back, and although I don't want to in front of Eustache and Stephan, I cry out in pain.

'Stop!' It's Ines, pushing into our burrow with Niklaus and Alard close behind her. 'Leave him alone.'

Eustache cracks the Oriflamme over me again. Everything is going hazy. I am all hot and cold at the same time. The Oriflamme is made of fire and it's branding me, like Papa does with cows. Why isn't Stephan saying anything? I thought I was the alpha fish. Why is he letting Eustache do this to me? I can only see the red of the Oriflamme, like blood drowning out the golden sun and the snow and everything else. All I can hear is the roaring of the blows in my ears. The embroidered tendrils of gold that burst out in wiggly lines from the sun wrap around my head and squeeze.

Finally, Stephan speaks. 'There is no danger. We must just close our eyes and march forward and the illusion of the storm will vanish. We must be pure of heart.'

He turns, and the children around us scramble out of their burrows. They believe him. They believe that the storm isn't real. That he can stop it. Why don't I believe him?

Maybe I *am* an apostate, whatever that is.

Stephan climbs onto his litter and four children lift it up. I start to cry. Ines comes over and tries to help me up, but I don't want to look at her. I am not worthy.

'Lead on,' says Stephan to Eustache.

'No!' says Ines. 'You'll kill them all.'

But they ignore her. The children all vanish behind them into the storm. Luc and David come over and press their hands against mine.

'I'm sorry, Gabby,' says Luc. 'But Stephan is our King.'

And then they are gone.

Alard clenches his fists and looks like he is going to cry. But after a moment, his shoulders fall and he follows.

Niklaus moves to follow as well.

'What are you doing?' says Ines.

Niklaus doesn't look at her. 'I can't leave them,' he says. 'They're my children too – all of them.'

'But you'll die.'

'I can't leave them,' he says again.

He takes a step forward and vanishes into the whirling white and grey and black.

Ines makes a noise that could be a scream or a sob, it is all scared and angry and hurt all in one. She looks down at me, and then after Niklaus. I close my eyes. She will stay with me. Even though I am not the alpha fish, Ines won't leave me here alone.

When I open my eyes she is gone.

I start to cry. Everyone has left me. Everyone. I am not a silvery fish. I am just a blind wriggling worm like the boys in Machery. I remember the boy with his black fingers and his black nose, and the prayers we said for him. Niklaus said that he would have a fast journey to the side of Our Lord. If I died right now, would I go straight to the Holy Land? Off this mountain? Could it really be that easy?

I close my eyes and I am a silvery fish again, swimming in the clearest of streams. The sun shines through the water onto my scales, warming me up and making flashes of blue and silver and gold in the water.

I'm not cold any more. My hands and feet don't ache, and I'm not stiff. I swish my tail back and forth and dive down to the bottom of the stream, where bright green weeds wrap themselves around me like a blanket, soft and warm. Then I wriggle up out of them and the weeds slide off my body, and I leave them behind as I push up, up, up through the water.

There is no ice in this stream. There is no snow. Only warmth and sunshine and . . . and something else.

There is something moving in the water ahead of me. Disappearing out of sight. Flashing silver tails.

It is Stephan and Niklaus and the other children.

You cannot be the alpha fish when there is only one of you. When there is only one, you become the first and the last.

I don't want to be last. I don't want to be left behind. I don't want to be alone.

There is a snuffle, and something warm presses against me. It's Fox-boy. I am not alone. I cry harder, and Fox-boy snuffles and twitches.

'Gabby,' he says. 'Gabby. Fambly.'

I think about Stephan and his secret smile. I think of Our Lord and His sad eyes and thin ribs. I think about the Saracen with their horns and smoke and fire.

'We can't stay here,' I tell Fox-boy. 'If we stay here alone, we will die.'

I know if we go out into the storm we will probably die too. But at least we will die trying to rescue Our Lord. We will die following Stephan, who is our King and can do Magic.

seventeen

For the first few seconds, the snow and ice make everything hurt with the most terrible pain. The places on my head and back where Eustache beat me with the Oriflamme hurt so much that I think I faint, because Fox-boy is pulling at me to make me stand up, and I didn't know I'd fallen down. I can't see anything, and I don't know if I am following Stephan or not because everything is white, white, white.

I know that with every step we could walk off a cliff and fall and die. But I keep walking forward. The hurt and the freezing is soon replaced with nothing. I can't feel my face or my feet or my hands. We just walk and walk, one step after the other. The storm screams terrible things at us and spits ice.

We keep walking.

I don't know if we've been walking for hours, or only for moments. Maybe we have crossed the mountains. Maybe we have only taken a few steps from our burrow. But through the white I see red.

A flash of red. It is so new after the endless whirl of white and black. Red means only one thing. Red means life, even if it is an ended life.

I walk towards it, and then stop so suddenly that Foxboy bumps into me and we nearly fall.

It's so hard to see, but I'm at the very edge of a cliff. The ground drops away suddenly, and there's just down, down, down, with no bottom. The red is down there, but not all the way down. Just a little bit. The snow spins around it in spirals like water in a fast river and, suddenly, I can understand what the storm has been screaming at me. It's screaming *gloria, gloria*.

I lie on my stomach and peer over the edge.

It's the Oriflamme. It's caught on a narrow ledge in the snow by the red and gold fabric. The wooden staff is hanging out over the drop, and I think it will fall any moment now.

Nearby, on a lower ledge, is Eustache, clinging to

the side of the cliff, his toes balanced on the thinnest of shelves. His face is cut, a stripe of red to match the Oriflamme. He sees me, and starts to cry.

I think how, so recently, it was me crying and bleeding, and him looking down at me.

'Gabriel,' he says, and it is the first time he has ever said my name. 'Help me, please. I slipped and the snow is so heavy. Nobody noticed. Nobody heard me. They just walked on.'

The Oriflamme trembles, and I think, this is it, it will fall. But it holds.

'Give me your hand,' says Eustache. 'Pull me up.'

I swallow. I think I could reach down there, but I might slip on the snow, and then we would both die.

I turn to Fox-boy, but he is lying on the snow on his side, jerking and twitching, his eyes all white and white coming from his mouth. He can't help me.

'Gabriel!' Eustache is yelling now. 'Don't be such a stupid coward. Don't you realise who I am?'

I think of how he beat me and spat at me and kicked dirt in my face. I remember how he took the Oriflamme and he took Stephan and whispered things in his ear and made him change. I remember the burning on my cheek when I met the noble in Briis-sous-Forges.

'He'll never take you back if you let me die,' says Eustache. 'You'll be tainted, black inside. Stephan will know.'

The Oriflamme slips and starts to fall, and without thinking, I reach down and snatch it. Eustache thinks I am reaching for him, and holds out his hand. I pull the Oriflamme up and Eustache's feet slip on the ledge and he scrabbles at the wall, but it is all ice and he loses his handhold and he falls.

My numb fingers curl around the wooden shaft of the Oriflamme, and I climb to my feet.

eighteen

We walk on, Fox-boy and I.

I do not think about Eustache. About what I did. Fox-boy was too busy twitching and shaking, and I don't know if he saw. By the time his eyes went back to brown and his mouth stopped leaking white foam, Eustache was gone and I was holding the Oriflamme. Maybe he thinks it was Magic.

And maybe it was. The Oriflamme makes me feel warm again, deep inside, even though the rest of me is cold. It has come back to me. Maybe it is what Our Lord wanted. Maybe it was a small Miracle of my very own.

I don't know where the rest of the army is. I don't know where Stephan is. They might not even be alive. But Fox-boy and I are going on, down the mountain.

The Oriflamme must be Magic, because after a while it stops snowing and the wind stops howling. Fox-boy and I carve out a hollow in the snow, and roll ourselves up in the Oriflamme and sleep for a while.

It is becoming difficult to tell whether I am awake or asleep. Everything seems sort of fuzzy, and I am tired after only a few steps. It gets harder to hold the Oriflamme up. My arms start to tremble and I have to lean it backwards across my shoulder.

I can't remember when I stopped feeling hungry.

The sun is blinding-bright on the snow and our crunching footsteps seem so loud it is like they are crunching inside my head.

Fox-boy walks a few steps in front of me. I think it must be time for a rest. We are sleeping a lot lately. But before I can say anything, Fox-boy cries out and scrambles forward. Has he found Stephan and the army?

I leap after him, and then I see it.

It is a tree. A twisted, old, bent-over tree that makes me think of the quince tree back at St Denis. But it is the first tree we have seen in days – weeks even.

I wrap my arms around its rough trunk and think of Ines, planting herbs in the abbey garden. I think of the smell of earth and sunshine, the sound of bees, the taste of bread.

And I cry and cry and cry.

Fox-boy cries too, a howling, barking cry.

There are more trees, and then bushes, and then our first glimpse of greenish-brown as the snow thins. Fox-boy and I try eating some of the leaves on the trees and bushes, but they make us sick.

When we come across a protected hollow and see a hut, I think I must be dreaming.

It is not a very sturdy hut – one of the walls is leaning out on an angle, and it looks like a good storm could push the whole thing over. But there are four walls and a roof and, best of all, smoke rising from a hole in the corner.

I knock on the door and wait. Fox-boy runs around in excited little circles.

I hear the jangling of a bell. Then a voice comes from inside that sounds like branches snapping.

'*Impuro!*' it says. '*Impuro!*'

I don't know what this means, but I am cold and want to sit by the fire. So I knock again.

The door to the little hut opens, and a man appears. Or is it a monster?

He is short and twisted, like the trees around his hut. He wears a sackcloth robe and carries a bell which he thrusts, clanging towards us. His skin is all wrinkled and lumpy, and I cannot tell how old he is. It has been so long since I saw another person apart from Fox-boy, and even longer since I saw a grown-up person. The hand that holds the bell is smooth and shiny, with only three fingers on it. His other hand has no fingers at all.

'*Impuro!*' he says again in his dry-sticks voice. '*Impuro!*'

'We just want to warm up by your fire,' I say. 'We've been lost in the mountains.'

The man stops ringing the bell and stares at me for a moment with milky eyes that are rimmed with red. I notice he has no eyelashes. Then he notices the Oriflamme in my hand, and makes the Holy Sign.

The inside of the hut is dark, and doesn't smell very nice. But it is warm, and Fox-boy immediately makes for the smoky little fire, curls up and falls asleep.

The old man busies himself with a pot that hangs over the fire, and soon hands me a bowl of hot broth. He doesn't seem to miss his fingers.

'Slowly,' he says, in my tongue. He speaks it as if he has not done so for many years.

I sip some of the broth, and it feels strange in my mouth. I'm not sure I remember what to do with it. But

I swallow and soon the most delicious warmth spreads through my body.

'Who are you?' I ask the dry-sticks man. 'What are you doing here all alone?'

'I'm dead,' says the man. 'A ghost.'

I look at the bowl in my hands. It is hard and solid and warm and real. This man gave me this bowl.

'You don't seem like a ghost,' I say.

He shrugs. 'I am,' he says. 'When I became a leper, I died. I stood in my own grave while a priest threw dirt on me and read in Latin. *Sis mortuus mondo, vivens iterum Deo.* Dead to the world, reborn to God.'

I have heard people talk about lepers. They have a disease that is very deadly. I wonder if I shall catch it from drinking the leper's broth.

He sees the look on my face and his laugh is like flames crackling wood.

'Don't worry,' he says. 'The Holy symbol of St Denis will protect you.' He jerks his head at the Oriflamme, which is resting by the door.

'How do you know it's from St Denis?' I ask.

'I know lots of things,' says the dry-sticks man. He looks a bit sad when he says this, which I think is strange. If I knew lots of things I'm sure I'd be happy because there wouldn't be so many questions.

I want to ask him all my questions. I want to ask him about Stephan and Our Lord and the Holy Land

and Niklaus and whether the children who died on the mountain really were black inside. But I don't know which question to ask first, so instead I ask if he knows anything about silvery fish.

He smiles, and I see gums and black teeth.

'Fish,' he says. 'Fish. The symbol of life. Of Our Lord. Of everything.'

I feel empty. That was me. The symbol of everything. The alpha fish. But not any more.

The dry-sticks man leans forward. 'It was once believed that pagan gods were born from the mouths of fishes.'

I wonder if he is being a heretic, and I'm glad that no one else is here to tell him to stop.

'In the east, people believe that dead souls live inside fish. Women wishing to birth a child eat fish in the hope that the dead soul will flow into her and spark new life.'

I imagine a silvery fish swimming into a woman's mouth and making a child grow inside her. I think of the wet, slippery brothers and sisters my Maman birthed, and I shiver.

'Why are you so interested in fish?' asks the dry-sticks man.

I tell him about Stephan and how he said I was the alpha fish. Then I tell him about the Children's Army and the Oriflamme and Eustache and the heretics who were killed in the village and about the mountain and the storm. I don't tell him about Eustache falling. The words don't come out.

'You want to fight the Saracen?' he asks.

'I don't know if I can,' I tell him. 'But I want to save Our Lord and the Holy Land.'

'But what if Our Lord doesn't want to be saved?' the man murmurs, almost to himself.

'Of course He does! Why wouldn't He?'

The man stares at the fire for a moment, frowning. 'I'm not sure we are the right ones to do the saving.' he says. 'Sometimes I think we are just as bad as the Saracen.'

'The Saracen are monsters!'

'As are all men. Our soldiers have not just killed the Saracen in this war. They have killed Judeans and pagans and heretics and Waldensians and Hussites. Many innocent lives have been lost under the guise of fighting the Saracen.'

I am not sure what to say. Is he telling the truth?

The dry-sticks man looks up from the fire and nods at me. 'But perhaps you are right,' he says. 'Perhaps our grown hands are so dirty with blood that it is only the tiny clean hands of children that can finally end this war.'

I look down at my hands. They are not so clean.

'Perhaps it is not the fishers of men who are to save us,' the man continues, 'but the fish itself. The alpha fish.'

'Except I don't think I am, any more,' I tell him. 'I lost the army. I let Stephan leave without me. I can't be the alpha fish without him.'

The dry-sticks man thinks about this. I listen to the rattling of his breathing and think he must be very wise, to have so many thoughts.

'You say you are the alpha fish,' he says at last.

'I thought I was,' I reply.

'And that you were the first to bear the Oriflamme.'

'Yes.'

The dry-sticks man looks at the Oriflamme by the door, and then stares into the fire.

'And the Oriflamme came back to you.'

'I found it. In the snow.'

He nods. 'You were destined to carry it.'

I breathe in. *Destined.* The Oriflamme is mine. It was right for me to rescue it instead of Eustache.

'But what if I can't find Stephan and the army?' I ask.

'You will,' he replies.

'How do you know?'

The dry-sticks man rubs at his face with his fingerless hand. 'Where is Stephan headed?'

'To the ocean. It's going to dry up so we can walk across.'

'And how is he going to do that?'

I shrug. 'I don't know. He knows secret Magic.'

The dry-sticks man smiles. 'I know,' he says. 'He needs something. A talisman.'

'The Oriflamme?'

'Yes. But not just the Oriflamme. You say you are the alpha fish.'

'Yes.' I am starting to tremble.

'Where do you find fish?'

I swallow. 'In water.'

'What kind of water?'

I think about what Stephan told us. About where we were going. 'The – the ocean?'

'Yes.' The dry-sticks man reaches out and his three fingers curl around my hand. 'Yes. You are his talisman. You are the alpha fish.'

And I know what I have to do.

nineteen

It is not difficult to find the army. As Fox-boy and I walk out of the leper's valley and climb the next crest, we see the world spread out below us.

Below are hills that turn into flat ground. There is rough, hairy green everywhere, but below I can see patchwork squares of farms and fields. And there, at the bottom of the mountain, is the army. I can barely make them out, but there is smoke coming from fires, and some tiny brown dots that move about.

Fox-boy does a little dance around in a circle. But I am still a bit frightened of what will happen when I return. Will they guess about Eustache? Will Stephan look inside me and know what I did?

I touch the red fabric of the Oriflamme for comfort, and remember what the dry-sticks man said. I am the alpha fish. I am his talisman.

We scramble down the mountain, chewing on strips of cured meat that the dry-sticks man gave us. Fox-boy tries to catch a rabbit, but he is not fast enough. I wish we had a bow and arrow, though I don't know if I could work one.

By the time we reach the camp where I saw the army, they have moved on. But it is not difficult to follow them now. They leave wide trails through the thick green forest, broken branches and trampled undergrowth.

We find them the next morning. The forest is very close here, so nobody sees me at first. I look through branches and I feel cold and a bit sick.

There are not many children left. I think there is maybe the same amount we had when we left St Denis. Maybe less. But that is counting all of the grey army as well. I see Luc, looking thin and sad and small, like a little boy. There is no David. Alard is here too, but I can't see any of the other nobles. Did they all die?

I can hear a strange noise. A screaming, angry noise.

I creep forward, and see Stephan's orange and gold robes. I let out a breath I didn't know I'd been holding, and tears fill my eyes and I think I might fall over with relief. He is safe. I want to run forward and throw myself to the ground and touch his ankles. But then I notice that the screaming, angry noise is coming from him. I move closer. Fox-boy seems nervous being around so many people after us being alone for what feels like such a long time, although I think it is only a few days. He walks very close to me, his shoulder pressed against mine.

Stephan looks different. His cheeks and throat are puffy and pasty, like bread dough. He looks fatter than he did before. He has two chins, and black pouches under his eyes.

Some of the thin, sad children notice me and Fox-boy and the Oriflamme. They stare with open mouths.

Stephan and Niklaus are facing each other. Both look angry. Niklaus's hair has grown longer since I first saw him. Now it wisps and curls over his forehead. It makes him look younger.

'The children are weak,' Niklaus is saying. 'We should rest here for a few days and let them recover.'

'No!' Stephan's voice is like a barking dog, high and sharp. 'If they cannot march, they are not blessed. We should just leave them here.'

'We are their leaders,' says Niklaus. 'We can not abandon them.'

'Stay, then.' Stephan turns and starts to walk away. 'I don't want you to be there when I part the ocean. Your pretend holiness will spoil the Magic.'

'You will never part the waters,' says Niklaus. There is something in his voice I have never heard before. Something black and red, like burning coals.

I look around for Ines, and see her standing nearby, looking fiercely from Stephan to Niklaus. My knees go wobbly and I have to stop myself from crying out, I am so happy to see her. She looks taller, and older, but that might just be because she is thinner. She is wearing her hair all curled up in a knot at her neck, the way the other Rhineland girls do. Blanchefleur is standing next to her, holding Ines's hand. Her golden hair is lank and thin, the blue ribbons gone. Her cheeks are hollow and her eyes are red from crying.

I lower the Oriflamme so it is tucked under my arm, and inch around to Ines. She turns and sees me and Fox-boy, and she opens her mouth, as if she wants to say something but has no words. It is good to see her, which is a surprise. She ruffles Fox-boy's hair, then touches my cheek and takes my hand so she has me on one side and Blanchefleur on the other. Fox-boy sits and rests his head against Ines's legs. Blanchefleur leans forward to catch my eye and smiles a wobbly, thin smile, then turns back to look at Niklaus and Stephan.

Stephan has stopped walking. He turns back and his

face is even blacker than Niklaus's. I am frightened, and squeeze Ines's hand.

'How dare you.' Stephan's voice is low and dangerous.

Niklaus's face is like stone. 'No,' he says. 'How dare *you*. How dare you dress in such fine robes when your children wear rags? How dare you feast like a king when your children starve? How dare you make them carry you over mountains when they are so weak they can barely stand? You are not chosen by Our Lord. You are not Holy or pious or blessed. You are weak and greedy and full of hate.'

I can see Stephan's fists curled tight. He is white all over and trembling.

'I. Am. Holy.' His teeth grit tight together. 'I. Am. Blessed.'

Niklaus's top lip curls. 'Liar,' he says. 'Charlatan.'

And then all of a sudden they are not Holy leaders, but children fighting. They yell and kick and hit and scratch, and they are like farm-boys.

Ines lets go of me and Blanchefleur. 'Stop!' she says, and runs forward to pull them apart. 'Stop!'

Stephan rakes his nails across Niklaus's face. Niklaus grabs a handful of Stephan's hair and pulls, and Stephan screams in pain and fury. Ines gets shoved aside by Stephan and she falls.

'Enough!' says a voice, and I am so very surprised to learn that it comes from me. I hear Blanchefleur's breath go hissing in. Fox-boy whimpers. I grab the Oriflamme and hold it high.

'Enough!' I say again.

They let go of each other and look up at the flapping red and gold. Stephan cries out.

'A ghost,' he says. 'It is a sign from Our Lord that I am the true leader. I am Holy.'

Niklaus looks at me too, but says nothing.

'I'm not a ghost,' I say. I'm about to say that I found the Oriflamme, and tell them about Eustache and the storm and the mountain. But I don't. Instead, I say, 'But I am a sign. I am the alpha fish.'

Everyone is staring at me. I take a deep breath. 'I am the alpha fish,' I say again. 'And the bearer of the Oriflamme.'

'Yes!' says Stephan. 'Yes! Tell them. Tell them that I am Holy.'

'You are Holy,' I say, and as I look at him I feel a sob of happiness rising in my throat, because I am near him again. I blink away tears, and hope that I can finish what I have to say before I start crying properly.

'You are Holy, and so is Niklaus,' I say. 'You are both chosen by Our Lord. You will both part the ocean. You will both lead us to the Holy Land.'

There is a long silence, and I watch Stephan's chest moving up and down.

'Very well,' he says at last. 'We will rest here today

and tonight, and leave tomorrow.'

Niklaus bows his head in a slow nod, and walks away. Ines follows him a few paces behind.

Stephan turns and leaves as well. I want to follow him, but then I remember that if it weren't for me, it would be Eustache following him. And I wonder again if he knows, if he can see it inside me. If he can see what I did.

I should not follow Stephan. I am not worthy.

twenty

It gets warm again as we travel south. But I am cold inside. Every morning I wake up and look at my fingers to see if the blackness inside me is starting to leak out. I know it will, sooner or later.

Whenever I close my eyes, I see Eustache on the ledge. Asking me for help. Every time I hold the Oriflamme, I think of how I reached for it instead of Eustache.

I don't talk to Stephan. I can't. He will know what I did, and he will hate me. And nothing in the world

Company of Angels

would be worse. I'd rather I never spoke to him again. At least this way I can still be near him.

There is a sort of peace between Niklaus and Stephan, as fragile as the bones of a bird. They do not speak to each other, but they do not fight. Stephan is still carried on the litter made from the red tent. The grey army are hunting again, and Stephan always takes the best meat for himself.

We pass through some small towns. The villagers come out and stare at us. They speak a strange tongue that even Niklaus struggles with, but when they see his three-pronged cross and the Oriflamme, they run forward to touch us and give us bread and milk.

Most days I walk with Fox-boy. Sometimes I walk with Ines, but she is very quiet. The mountain changed her. Or Niklaus. I'm not sure. She follows him wherever he goes, helping the sick and the wounded. She is teaching Blanchefleur to collect herbs to make treacles. Sometimes Fox-boy and I go with them and Ines tells us about plants. I like helping. We make a treacle from lettuce, briony, poppies, henbane and the juice of hemlock.

'Careful,' warns Ines as I wipe the black juice onto my tunic. 'Hemlock is deadly.'

'Then why are we feeding it to the sick people?' I ask. 'Won't it kill them?'

Ines glances at Blanchefleur and raises her eyebrows.

Blanchefleur shakes her head. 'In just the right amounts,' she explains, 'mixed with the right things, it can cure many illnesses.'

Ines nods and smiles.

She tells us that a person's body is made of four humours, like the four elements.

She spits on the ground. 'That is water,' she says. 'Earth is melancholia, the black bile that lives deep in the belly. Air is blood. Fire is the yellow bile you see when you are sick.'

I remember being sick and tasting the burning feeling in my throat. It *is* like fire, even though it is wet.

'When you are sick,' says Ines, 'it's because the humours become unbalanced. Too much black bile and you will be sad. Too much yellow and you will be sick. The treacles help even them all out again.'

I think of the black fingers of the children on the mountain. I think of the blackness inside me because of what I did. Somehow I don't think that my blackness can go away with one of Ines's treacles.

Ines pounds the herbs together with her wooden pestle. 'Of course,' she says. 'This is not a real treacle.'

I wrinkle my nose and Blanchefleur giggles. Whatever it is, it doesn't smell very good.

'Brother Samuel told me that a real treacle has over sixty ingredients, including the roasted skin of vipers and the gall of a boar.'

'Which part of a boar is the gall?' asks Blanchefleur.

'Deep inside,' replies Ines, putting her hand on her stomach. 'It's where the yellow fire bile is stored.'

'How do you get it out?' I ask. 'Without the boar getting angry?'

Blanchefleur giggles again, and I think that maybe she is not so bad after all. Ines glares at me, but she is smiling at the same time, so I know she is not really angry.

'It takes forty days to make the treacle,' Ines says, 'and then twelve years before it's ready.'

Surely if someone's sick, they can't wait for twelve years for their medicine.

'It becomes the stuff that Angels are made of,' says Ines. 'They call it *quintessence*.'

This country is very hilly, but nothing like the mountains behind us. They look smaller every day as we travel away from them. We are getting our strength back, eating rabbits and nuts and wild greens. No children have died for a few days now.

I stay away from Stephan. I am frightened of what he will say when I tell him about Eustache and the Oriflamme. And also, I am a little afraid of him. He looks so different, with his bread-dough skin and dark pouches under his eyes. He doesn't really talk to anyone any more. He just sits on his litter and mutters to himself, frowning and clutching a wooden cup.

'He says it is gold,' whispers Blanchefleur to me. 'He says it is the golden cup that Our Lord once drank from.'

I look at Stephan, his hands wrapped around the cup and his face looking down into it.

'Maybe it is,' I tell Blanchefleur. 'Maybe you have to be truly Holy to see it properly.'

Blanchefleur shrugs. 'Maybe,' she says doubtfully.

'Gabby!' It is Fox-boy, coming bounding over the hill where he has been running ahead of us. 'Gabby!'

He is panting and trembling, his eyes wide. I think for a moment he is going to fall over and twitch again, but he doesn't. He grabs my hand and pulls.

'Come,' he says. 'Hurry!'

I let him pull me forward, up to the top of the hill.

'Lookit,' he says, pointing, as proud as can be.

And I look, and see the ocean for the first time.

twenty-one

The water is blue and beautiful and I think it might go on forever. It makes me feel very small. I glance at Stephan and I know he is thinking about the day when he will call on his Magic and the water will dry up. There is a lot of water. I hope his Magic is strong.

Genoa is busy and bustling and smells of fish and salt. The streets are narrow and the buildings unfamiliar, built tall and thin in black and white stone. There are people everywhere, speaking many tongues that I don't understand. Some of them are dark-skinned and wear red or blue robes. There are monks dressed in white. Everyone stares at us, then they weep and applaud.

One little girl dances out in front of us and throws flowers under her feet, singing in a high, sweet voice. She curtsies and speaks some words we do not understand.

'Hello,' I say to her.

'Hello,' she repeats in my tongue, and then dissolves into giggles and scampers away.

We walk through a narrow passageway and find ourselves in an open square that holds a church. It looks a lot like the church at Saint Denis – square with a tower on one side, and three arched doorways in front. But this church isn't made of brown-grey stone. It is striped in black and white. It is the strangest thing I've ever seen. On the steps, two stone lions sit and look fierce.

There are monsters everywhere. Stone creatures cling to the outsides of buildings and crouch over gutters. Brass sea-monsters with curved tails hang from the middle of wooden doors. High up on a wall, there is a picture of a green dragon with a knight holding a spear. Around the corner, there is another wall-painting, this time of Our Lord wearing a spiky wreath on His head, His eyes sadder than ever.

We walk through the streets and everyone cheers and throws flowers at us and people run forward to grab Stephan and Niklaus's robes and kiss the hems. I wonder how they know who we are.

A group of richly dressed men step out in front of us. One wears a heavy gold chain around his neck. He has tiny eyes and a large, soft mouth.

'Welcome,' he says. 'The citizens of Genoa welcome the Children's Army.'

His voice is low and soft, and he speaks our tongue slowly and carefully.

Stephan and Niklaus bow their heads to him.

'We have heard all about you,' says the man. 'Your story has travelled faster than you have. We are all praying for your success in the Holy Land, and will do all that we can to assist.'

Both Stephan and Niklaus begin to speak at once, and then stop, glaring at each other. Then Niklaus gestures to Stephan and takes a half step back.

'My thanks,' says Stephan to the man. 'My thanks for your welcome, and the generosity of your citizens. Please, tell them to gather on the shore tomorrow at dawn, because there they will witness the greatest Magic of our time.'

The man's eyes widen. 'It is true then? You will part the very ocean?'

Stephan smiles. 'I shall,' he says.

The man bows low, his heavy chain clanking on the ground. Stephan holds out his hand for the man to kiss.

We gather bread and cakes and fruit and wine from the people, who weep with happiness as they press gifts into our hands. I am not sure I deserve gifts, but I take them anyway.

We march through the city to the docks, and then turn and walk down beside the ocean until we reach a stretch of white sand.

It's getting dark, so we light fires and sit around them eating our cakes and drinking the wine. It is sour and I don't like it very much, but I still drink it. It makes my head feel fuzzy, and something moves around in my stomach that I haven't felt before.

I get up and walk away from the fire. Nobody notices me leave. Fox-boy is asleep, along with most of the other children. Luc is talking quietly with Alard. Blanchefleur sits alone, staring into the fire.

I need to talk to Ines. I can't see her, but I think she's probably over with Niklaus and the Rhineland children. I cross over a dark patch of sand and into the light of the next fire. No Ines. No Niklaus. Nor at the next fire, or the next.

Then I see them, at a fire a little apart from the others. Niklaus is kneeling in the sand with his head bowed over a basin. He dips a knife into the water and holds it up. Firelight glints off it, and I see that his hand is trembling. He stares at it for a moment.

Ines is standing behind him, and she reaches forward and takes the knife. He holds on for a moment, and then releases his grasp, turning round to stare at Ines like she is an Angel, or a monster. Then he turns back to the fire. Slowly and carefully, Ines starts to shave Niklaus's head.

The firelight dances over them and strange shadows walk wild across their faces. I am close enough to them that I can hear the scrape of the knife over Niklaus's head, but it is dark outside the circle of firelight, so they cannot see me.

Niklaus is staring into the fire like he is hoping it will tell him a secret. His eyes burn red and blue and gold. Ines wipes a cloth over Niklaus's head, and then, very gently, kisses his brow.

I turn away. I cannot talk to Ines now. I turn and head away from the fires into the darkness.

I take off my boots and feel the sand between my toes. It's soft and scratchy and wonderful. The water is black and shining and it makes this roaring sound and then a *shh, shh* sound as it creeps up the sand. It reminds me of the sound of Stephan's feet as he walked along the dusty road the first time I saw him.

I go and stand at the edge of the water and feel it tickle my feet. It's cold and fresh and smells like salt and promises. Stars glitter above me, light leaking in from the Holy Land, bright and beckoning, and the moon sings *soon, soon, soon*. I should feel happy now.

In the white moonlight, I see a figure standing alone on the sand, further away from the camp. I don't need to see him properly – I know it is Stephan.

And I know it is time to tell him what I did.

As I approach, I see his body stiffen, and then relax when he sees it's me.

'Gabriel,' he says. 'My alpha fish.'

I feel happy at his words and then bitter as something stabs into the blackness in my stomach. I won't be his alpha fish for much longer.

Stephan looks out over the black water.

'Are you frightened?' I ask him. 'Of the Magic?'

He sighs. 'You know,' he says. 'Once everything was water. Everywhere.'

'Where were the people?' I ask.

'On a boat,' says Stephan. 'There were only a few, and their animals.'

I have heard this story before, about the boat and the animals and the rain. But when I think about it now, there are questions that weren't there before. Where did they build the boat? Where did the wood come from, if there was no land? Where did all the ocean go when the land came? But I don't ask them, because I don't want Stephan to think that I am questioning what he says.

'They had to wait,' says Stephan. 'For it to stop raining. So the water would go away.'

I imagine being on a boat, water underneath, water falling from above. It would be a bit like being a fish.

'Our Lord was angry,' says Stephan. 'He wanted to wash the world clean of all the bad people.'

'And the animals?' I ask. 'Were they all bad too?'

I'm not sure if it's possible for an animal to be bad. Not bad in the kind of way that Stephan is talking about. Not the kind of bad that would let Eustache die.

'Yes,' says Stephan. 'Everything was evil. It all had to begin again.'

'But not the fish,' I say, and he looks at me.

'The fish?' he asks.

'The fish would have stayed. They could swim in the water. They wouldn't get washed away. They didn't need the boat.'

Stephan stares at me. 'No,' he says finally. 'Not the fish.'

There is a trembling in his voice as he speaks. He is frightened. He is frightened of using his Magic tomorrow to part the ocean. I want to tell him it will be all right and that he will be able to do it. But what right do I have?

'I need –' My throat goes all dry. I lick my lips and clear my throat. I tremble and I think I might be sick. Maybe it is the blackness coming out. I imagine vomiting all the blackness out in a big sticky lump. I wish it was that easy to get rid of.

'I'm sorry,' I whisper. 'I'm sorry. I'm black inside.'

Stephan shakes his head. I think he must be very disappointed in me.

'No,' he says at last. 'No. No.'

Then he looks at me. The white parts of his eyes are very white. 'You are not black inside.'

'But I am,' I say, 'I. . .'

I still can't even say it out loud. I swallow and try again. 'Eustache –'

'No.'

'But Stephan –'

His face goes blank.

'My Lord,' I stutter and start to cry. 'I'm sorry.'

I fall down to the sand and lay my forehead against his ankles. They are very hot, even though the night is cool. His skin is burning to touch. Stephan flinches where I touch him.

'You have no blackness,' he says. 'Because you are in the Army of Children. All your wickedness is forgiven. Everything you do is to further our Holy Purpose.'

I feel tears dripping into the sand. How can I be part of the Army of Children and the Holy Purpose if I let Eustache die? And what about the children that died on the mountain? They were in the Army of Children too. Why weren't they forgiven?

'This blackness you speak of,' says Stephan. 'Was it motivated by spite, or hate, or greed?'

I don't say anything, but my heart cries out *yes, yes, yes*. All of those things.

Stephan bends down and kneels before me in the sand. I look up and I see a whisper of his old secret smile.

My heart aches and fresh tears drip.

'Or did you do what you did to protect our Holy Purpose?' he says, his voice gentle.

He knows. He knows what I did. He knows that I saved the Oriflamme instead of Eustache. He knew all along. I feel foolish. Of course he knew. He is our King. He can talk to Our Lord. He is going to make the ocean dry up tomorrow.

'Did you, Gabriel? he says. 'Did you serve the Higher Purpose?'

I wipe my eyes and sand gets all mixed in with the tears and scratches my cheeks. Did I? Was I not greedy and hateful at all, but brave and noble? Was I really serving Our Lord all along? Maybe that's why I did it. Maybe that's why Eustache was so mean to me, so that when the time came for me to choose, I chose the Oriflamme. Maybe it was what Our Lord wanted.

I blink the sand out of my eyes and nod. Yes. Yes. I am still here. I am still a part of the Higher Purpose. I am still the alpha fish.

Stephan smiles at me, and it's like I'm flying again. I feel warm and safe and free.

'I need you, Gabriel,' he says. 'I need you to believe in me.'

I think about tomorrow, about what Stephan is going to do, and I nod.

twenty-two

Dawn comes cold and shivery. The clouds are low and grey, and the wind has stirred the ocean into tall waves.

I don't think it is beautiful any more. It is a hungry monster that roars and keeps rushing up the beach to eat us all. I don't want to walk on the ocean floor. What if Stephan's Magic runs out and the ocean swallows us all up before we reach the Holy Land?

Everyone is quiet and trembling. We're all watching Stephan and Niklaus. Stephan frets and won't eat his breakfast and snaps at people. Niklaus is sitting on the sand away from us all, his head bowed in prayer and his lips moving as he whispers.

The only person who isn't jittery is Ines. She is all smiles and calm.

'You're not nervous?' I ask her.

She shakes her head. 'What is there to be nervous about?' she says.

'What if it doesn't work?' I say. 'What if they can't make the water dry up?'

Ines looks at me like I'm crazy. 'Of course it will work,' she says. 'You just have to believe.'

She looks at Niklaus, and her eyes fill up with something as huge and powerful as the ocean.

I do believe. I do. But I have so many questions. I follow Ines around as she checks on the sick children and ask her all my questions.

How does it work? What will they do? Will all the water dry up? Will it just move to the side and make a tunnel for us? What happens to all the fish? What if the Magic runs out?

Ines has no answers. She just smiles and says, 'You must trust Niklaus. He will take us to the Holy Land.'

I shiver as a cold breath of wind blows in off the water. I wish I was as sure as Ines.

The people of Genoa gather on the sandy hills behind us. There are thousands of them, dressed in bright clothes and waving coloured banners.

The children stand facing the water. Even though so many of us died in the Alps, we are still an army. I see Fox-boy standing with Luc, their shoulders pressed together. I see Blanchefleur holding Alard's hand, her eyes wet with tears.

I hold the Oriflamme high. It is ragged now, torn and stained from its adventures. But it is still red as blood, and gold as the sun. Ines holds Niklaus's strange three-pronged cross.

Stephan and Niklaus stand side-by-side. For a moment I am afraid they will argue about who is going to do the Magic, but they don't. They just walk forward to the water together.

The waves are pounding down onto the sand in a thumping roar and great sprays of foam and water. Niklaus and Stephan look very small. Then the Genoans start to sing the *gloria* song, and I sing too and so do all the children. Suddenly the waves aren't just crashing and banging, they are roaring *gloria! Gloria!*

I feel every hair on my body stand on end. It's going to happen. It's really going to happen. I grip the Oriflamme so tightly I think I will break it. I hold my breath.

There is a huge growl of thunder, and the sky lights up with flashes of lightning. The Genoans gasp, and then keep singing.

Gloria!

Gloria!

I feel the *gloria*s pour out of me like the purest water. I am a silvery fish, swimming in the clear water. I am a soaring bird and a shining star.

Gloria! Gloria!

As the thunder rolls and roars and the ocean pounds, Stephan and Niklaus raise their hands up to the sky. It lights up as if in answer with great blue and silver forks of lightning.

I think I might tear apart, I am so shaky. I close my eyes and feel the wind and the water and the *gloria*s flowing through me. I feel it happen. I am here. I am really here.

I hear the water roar louder and fiercer than ever, and I know it is happening now. I know that this is it. I know it more than I have ever known anything before.

I open my eyes, ready for the wall of water rushing away from the sandy ocean floor.

But it hasn't happened yet.

The people keep singing. The ocean keeps roaring. Niklaus and Stephan keep their hands raised to the sky.

But nothing happens.

It must take a while. This is such a huge Magic. It will take time.

After an hour, the Genoans have all stopped singing. Most of them have gone back into the city. Some of them yell bad words at us. Others wait and pray.

After two hours, some of the children wander off too, in search of leftover food from last night's feast.

I wait. Ines waits. Niklaus and Stephan remain down by the water.

It starts to rain, great fat icy drops that slide down my face and onto my neck. Soon, the Oriflamme is soaked through and droops down onto its wooden pole and drips water onto my head.

And still we wait.

My fingers go numb, and I think I must have fallen asleep standing up for a while, because soon it is growing dark and we are still here, still waiting.

I hear jeers and shouts from behind us. I don't know if it's the children or the Genoans. I also hear sobs and howls.

Fox-boy comes and brings Ines and me some soggy bread and an apple each. I eat mine hungrily, but Ines refuses hers. She doesn't take her eyes off Niklaus.

It is fully dark now. The rain and wind have stopped. The ocean is still there, still wet. Some of the children have found dry wood and have lit fires higher up the beach. They look warm. I can smell meat cooking. I clear my throat.

'Ines?' I say. My voice sounds very loud.

Ines ignores me.

'Ines?' I say again. 'How long do we wait?'

She says nothing.

I jam the Oriflamme into the sand so it stays up on its own, and sit down. My muscles ache from standing all day. Fox-boy brings me a blanket, and some hot mulled wine. As I start to grow warm again, my eyelids droop and I fall asleep.

When morning comes, they are still there. Ines, Stephan and Niklaus. Waiting.

The storm has completely gone, and the sun is warm and the breeze fresh.

There are no children waiting any more. They sit around campfires, or wander off into the city. Some of them cry and snuffle and others sneer.

Fox-boy comes and sits by me. He has sand on his nose.

'What now?' he asks.

I shake my head. I don't know. Part of me still wants to believe they can do it. That it takes time to make the Magic work. But deep down I know. I know that they have failed. I know that the Children's Army is over and that we will never get to the Holy Land.

When the sun has climbed high into the sky, Niklaus turns from the ocean and walks away, his head bowed. He disappears into the sand dunes. Ines drops the three-pronged cross and crumples into the sand.

After a few moments, Stephan turns as well, and makes his way back up the beach towards us.

He sees me, and smiles. 'Don't worry,' he murmurs. 'It will work. It will. Maybe tomorrow.'

twenty-three

It doesn't. It doesn't work tomorrow, or the next day.

Niklaus has gone. Nobody has seen him since he walked away from the ocean.

Ines doesn't speak. Her face is white and empty. I find myself wishing she'd cry and scream like she did at the heretic village. But she doesn't. She won't even eat or drink anything.

Blanchefleur, Fox-boy and I take turns sitting with her. I hold her hand, but she is like a statue. Sometimes I think she might be dead, but she still blinks and breathes.

'Her heart is broken,' whispers Blanchefleur to me. Her voice trembles and she looks thin and pale.

I wonder which of the four humours is the one that looks after a broken heart. I wonder if there is a treacle that can fix her.

Stephan spends all day by the water, watching and trying. Each morning when I wake up, I have a spark of hope that he will have done it during the night, that we will awake to a great tower of water with a tunnel inside, and Stephan will be standing at its mouth with his secret smile and his arrow-blue eyes. But each morning that spark gets smaller.

The Oriflamme and the three-pronged cross are still stuck in the sand where Ines and I stood. They are starting to lean and sag.

Some of the children make rods and lines and we catch fish to cook on our beach fires. The people of Genoa no longer cheer and press fruit and cakes into our hands. We are sick of fish, and some boys are stealing milk and bread and cheese.

I walk along the beach, testing to see how far I will go before I turn back, afraid of being alone.

One day I come across Blanchefleur. She is sitting with her knees pulled up to her chin, crying silently.

'Are you all right?' I ask.

She starts and looks up at me, her enormous blue eyes made all the prettier by their tears.

'No.'

I sit down beside her.

'I want to go home,' she says.

I pat her arm. 'Then you should,' I say. 'You should go home. There are children leaving every day. I'm sure you could travel with them.'

She shakes her head. 'No,' she says. 'I can't ever go home.'

'Why?'

Blanchefleur starts to cry again, harder this time. 'It's my fault,' she whispers.

'What do you mean?'

She turns and looks at me. 'Stephan failed because of me. Because of something I did – Something he did.'

I shake my head. I don't understand.

'He said that the Saracen would die as soon as we set foot on the soil of the Holy Land, right?'

I nod. Blanchefleur drags a hand across her wet cheeks and sniffles.

'Because of our innocence and purity, right?'

I nod again.

'Well,' says Blanchefleur. 'I'm not innocent and pure any more. And neither is Stephan.'

I still don't understand, but Blanchefleur keeps talking, big fat tears rolling down her cheeks.

'I didn't want to,' she says. 'But he said he needed it. He said it would be all right. He said it didn't count, because it was what Our Lord wanted. He said we'd be safe . . .'

She breaks off in another flood of tears. I pat her arm again. 'I'm sure you're mistaken,' I say.

'Then why didn't it work? Why didn't the water part?'

I stare at her. I have no answers.

On the fifth day, a group of well-dressed Genoans approach us. One of them is the man with the golden chain who greeted us when we arrived. He smiles sadly at Stephan with his soft mouth as his shoes sink into the sand.

'I am sorry,' he says to Stephan. 'Sorry that your mission has failed.'

Failed. Everyone seems to sag a little when we hear that word. We failed. Our Lord will have to suffer on. The Saracen will stay in the Holy Land. Because we failed. The man turns and raises his voice to speak to us all.

'You have all come so very far from your homes,' the man says. 'And I know the return journey seems impossible.'

Some of the children start to cry. We hadn't considered a home journey. I imagine having to cross the mountains again, and panic rises in my throat. I can't do it. I can't go back there again.

'But all is not lost,' says the man. 'I have come to offer you a new home, here in Genoa. Your courage and determination is admirable, and we'd be happy to welcome you as new citizens.'

Stay? Here in Genoa? I think about what it would be like, looking every day out onto the ocean that never parted. Seeing our failure. I think I would prefer to face the mountains again.

'We have families that can take in the younger children,' the man says. 'And we can find work for the older ones.'

He makes a little bow to Stephan. 'I'll leave you to discuss.'

He and the other men walk away, the ends of their robes trailing in the sand. Some of the younger children go scampering after them. I suppose they miss having a mother and father. I suppose I do too. I miss Maman and Papa. I miss the river and Maman's apple-cake and waking up in the morning knowing exactly what the day will hold.

After a few hours, Luc follows them. He doesn't say goodbye, he just glances at me and ducks his head. I think he feels guilty for leaving us, but I understand. He needs a family.

But I could never leave Stephan. Never.

I wake in the middle of the night with a jolt. Stephan is crouching over me, his face almost touching mine. His breath is sweet and his hands are hot on my arms. He's breathing heavily and his eyes look wide and vacant.

'Angel,' he mutters. 'Fish. Ghost. Help me.'

I try to sit up, but Stephan shoves me back down and bares his teeth.

'Why have you failed me?' he asks. 'Is it you?'

'Stephan,' I say. 'I don't understand.'

He grabs my collar and pushes me down into the sand. My head smacks against the ground with a thump and my breath goes whooshing out of my chest.

'It's your fault, Angel fish,' he says, pushing harder. 'Your fault I am failing. You.'

I gasp in air. My chest aches and my head throbs. 'No. I'm no Angel. You're tired.'

'Angel.' Stephan stops pushing me, and leans forward, pressing his forehead against mine. Our noses touch and his eyelashes brush mine. 'Angel fish. Ghost.'

All I can see are his eyes, as large as the sky. They glisten darkly, but I know that if it were daylight they would be arrow-blue.

He makes a noise that I feel vibrate in my chest. It is the sound that a bird makes when you hit it with a stone, just before it falls.

'Why won't you help me?' he asks. He shakes and makes the noise again. It is an animal noise, wild and frightening. He draws a great shuddering breath then the sobs come fast, coughing and choking.

'Angel. Angel. Angel.'

I wish I were an Angel. I wish I could help him. I wish I could give him the Magic he needs to part the ocean. I grasp his arms and stare into the eyes that completely fill my vision.

'I believe in you,' I say. I think this might be a lie.

'Angel,' says Stephan, his voice hoarse.

Tears drip from his eyes and run down his eyelashes, then mine, until they drop into my eyes. The salty water stings. I blink and it's like drinking with my eyes, swallowing his tears. They are hot and salty and I hope that they can wash away my doubt, and his.

twenty-four

Today, seven ships sail into Genoa harbour. They have square, white sails, and glide through the water. I think of fish and birds. They are beautiful.

Maybe half the children have gone back to Genoa. There are less than one thousand of us now.

Stephan doesn't speak to me about what happened last night. I think he probably doesn't even remember. His eyes are red and he is shaking. He mutters constantly to himself and twitches. I take him some fresh water to drink, but he dashes the bowl from my hands with a growl.

Company of Angels

I am not offended. I can still feel Stephan's tears burning inside me. I don't know what this means. I don't know why we have failed. But I know it's not over yet. It can't be.

I spend each day going between Stephan and Ines, trying to help them. Ines is eating now, and there is a bit of colour in her cheeks. But she still doesn't speak.

Fox-boy spends most of his time chasing seagulls on the beach, but today he comes and lies down in the sand and rests his head against Ines's legs and looks up at her with big eyes.

'Ines,' he whispers. 'Ines. Ines.'

Ines's eyes fill with tears and she cries silently. She wraps her fingers around the silver badges pinned to her dress.

I sit down beside her and put my arms around her and she sobs onto my shoulder. Now I have Stephan's tears inside, and Ines's outside.

When the afternoon shadows grow long, two men come to us. They are wearing simple leather breeches and white linen shirts, but their boots look expensive. The tallest man has black hair cut around his shoulders, and a black and grey beard that creeps down over his chin and thick neck. His chin is large and square and juts out. His eyes slope down at the outside corners, which makes him look like he is sorry about something.

'Excuse me,' he says. 'Which is Stephan of Cloyes?'

He speaks my tongue with the same strangeness as the people from Genoa, a sort of sing-song voice that is very different to the clipped, blunt way that Niklaus speaks.

I look at him, wondering what he wants. I look at the other man, who is fairer and fatter. He has thinning hair pulled back and tied at the nape of his neck. His cheeks bulge and his nose is red and shiny. His skin is rough and speckled with tiny holes. His lips part in a smile and he huffs a bit from walking across the sand.

It is the smiling man who convinces me that they mean no harm.

'I'll take you to him,' I say.

Stephan is sitting on the damp sand where the ocean rushes in and out. Every now and then the water surges in and swirls around his legs, but he doesn't seem to notice.

The two men sink to their knees and lean forward to touch their foreheads to the wet sand. Then they sit back up again. The fat man struggles a bit, and brushes sand from his hands.

'Stephan of Cloyes,' says the black-haired man. 'News of your Holy Mission has reached far. We are here to offer our humble assistance.'

Stephan doesn't turn. He just stares out at the water.

'I am Hugh the Iron,' says the black-haired man. 'This is William the Pig.'

The other man nods and smiles even wider. 'We are merchants,' he says. 'Shipping merchants.'

Stephan ignores them.

The two men look at one another.

'Tell him,' says the fat man under his breath.

The black-haired man licks his lips. 'We have sinned,' he says. 'Terrible sins.'

The Pig-man nods. 'We heard that if you join the fight against the Saracen, all your sins are forgiven.'

'We are pious,' says the Iron-man. 'We love Our Lord very deeply. We never meant to sin.'

'We're sorry for what we did,' says the Pig-man. 'Let us atone. Let us help you.'

'What did you do?' I ask. 'What was your sin?'

Hugh the Iron looks over his shoulder at me, but doesn't reply. William the Pig scratches his chin and shrugs.

'Terrible things,' he says with a wave of his hand.

'Lord Stephan,' says Hugh. 'We are here to help you. We have seven ships that are ready to sail. We can carry you and your army of children. Our ships will cut through the ocean and deliver you to the Holy Land.'

I frown. Really? These men can really take us to the Holy Land? Just like that? We don't have to pay them or anything?

I wonder what it was that they did that was so wrong they need to do this to make up for it. I know that seven ships must be expensive. And why can't they tell us what terrible things they did? They must be very terrible, and if that is true, then perhaps we shouldn't trust them.

But I did a terrible thing, too. And Stephan trusts me.

I wonder what Niklaus would say to these men. I wonder if he would trust them. I wonder what Ines would say, if she was here. I consider running and fetching her, but I don't want to leave Stephan alone with William and Hugh.

I look at Stephan, who continues to stare at the grey waves.

'We can leave tomorrow morning,' says William. 'You could be at the feet of Our Lord in twenty nights.'

Did Stephan hear? Perhaps this was what Our Lord wanted all along. Perhaps this has been a test. Perhaps it was a test to find out which of us are truly worthy. The children that left to stay in Genoa failed. But we are pure and true, and we will go to the Holy Land!

Stephan raises his head. I hold my breath.

And he starts to laugh, softly at first, but then louder and louder. He scrambles to his feet and jumps in the air, and dances around still laughing. He grabs me by the tunic and spins me round, and then runs up and down the beach, whooping and screaming.

Hugh the Iron and William the Pig look at each other.

'Thank you,' I say to them. Stephan has convinced me. He trusts them, so I trust them.

They turn to me. William the Pig grins, and I grin back.

'It is our pleasure,' he says. 'We are proud and grateful to help the Army of Children.'

Stephan comes running back up the beach, splashing and kicking the rushing water so it flies up in glittering droplets. A larger wave knocks him off his feet, and he falls to hands and knees, still laughing. I can see tears streaming down his face. I feel his tears inside me burning.

We're going to the Holy Land.

twenty-five

It is a bit frightening being on a ship. It creaks and moves, and I hope it will all stay together until we get to the Holy Land.

There's a big space under the ship's decking where we children are all squeezed in together.

Hugh the Iron and William the Pig have painted red crosses on the sails of the ships, in honour of us and our mission. Our ship has the Oriflamme tied to the mast with a piece of rope. One of the other ships has a sail painted with a three-pronged cross for Niklaus and the grey army, even though there are only a few of them remaining and no one has heard from Niklaus.

Ines is here with me, as is Fox-boy, and Stephan of course. Fox-boy is chasing rats around the hold, and knocking over other children and getting into trouble.

Blanchefleur is with Alard on one of the other ships. Next time we see them, we'll be in the Holy Land.

I wasn't sure at first if Ines would come with us. She won't look at Stephan, and holds her hands over her ears when he speaks. When he draws near, she moves away.

'You could stay,' I said to her on the dock. 'You could stay in Genoa. Find a family.'

'No,' she said, taking my hand. She is speaking again, although not very much. 'No, I'll stay with you.'

I squeezed her hand. 'Why didn't you go with him?' I asked. 'With Niklaus?'

She shook her head. 'Because it was lies,' she said. 'All lies.'

Stephan has recovered from his trial on the beach. He's now eating full meals every day – I make sure he's had enough to eat before the other children get their dinner, which is usually just stale bread and strips of dry meat. His cheeks are pink now, and he has begun speaking to us again. He tells us long stories about Our Lord and the Holy Land. Sometimes he stops in the middle of a thought and stares at nothing. I think that as we approach the Holy Land, he grows closer to Our Lord. He can't have much time or energy for us.

We don't see much of William the Pig and Hugh the Iron. They have their own cabin at the back of the ship. Sometimes they come down to the hold where we are all squashed together and count us. I can usually smell drink on them, and their eyes are red.

I often wonder what they did that was so terrible.

I remember what Stephan said about Eustache and me and the Holy Purpose. Perhaps it is the same with these men. Perhaps they were supposed to do the terrible thing that they did so that they would need to bring us to the Holy Land.

Stephan seems to think this is the case. He tells us a story about how Our Lord was once tested and had to sit on a hill for forty days and forty nights without food or water. He got tempted by devils and monsters, but He was strong. Stephan speaks often of his own test, and about the monsters that came out of the ocean to torment him.

I don't remember seeing any monsters, but maybe only Stephan could see them, like the golden cup.

Stephan then speaks of Hugh the Iron and William the Pig. About how they were sent from Our Lord. He says that when Our Lord told him that he would part the water, He meant that the ships would cut through the ocean as we sailed to the Holy Land.

After three days, clouds rush in and close over our heads. It starts to rain and the waters grow high and fierce.

The ship is shuddery. It makes my head spin and my stomach twist until I vomit great lumps of burning yellow bile everywhere.

'Too much fire,' says Ines. 'Your humours are out of balance.'

I spit. 'How can I possibly have too much fire?' I say. 'There is water everywhere. I am wet all the time.'

Ines laughs, and I am so happy to hear it that I almost don't mind feeling sick. 'It's not like that,' she says. 'It doesn't matter what's happening on the outside. It's what's inside.'

Fox-boy scrambles down the ladder and flops at my feet. He is sopping wet.

'Where have you been?' asks Ines.

Fox-boy raises his head. 'Olly-flamb,' he says. 'Checking the Olly-flamb.'

I think about the Oriflamme flapping wetly in the storm. It will protect us.

'Listen!' It is Stephan, his eyes bright. 'Can you hear them? The Angels? They sing to us. Sing us towards the Holy Land.'

I listen, but all I can hear is the sound of water.

Hugh and William come down into the hold and count us again.

'We're near the island of Sardinia,' says Hugh. 'There are reefs. It's very dangerous.'

'You must pray to Our Lord, children,' says William. 'Pray that He will deliver us safely to the Holy Land.'

Hugh glances at William with his eyebrows up. William shrugs.

'He will,' says Stephan. 'Don't fear. We will be safe. I can hear His voice. He says that we are blessed and pure. He says that we will reach the Holy Land.'

Ines holds my shoulder as I throw up again. I don't feel blessed or pure. I feel sick and miserable. Fox-boy's fingers brush across my brow, cold and whispering.

The hold is stinking and filthy and I think that maybe crashing open on a reef might not be so bad. At least then there'd be some fresh air.

The ship rolls so far to one side that I think we'll tip over and drown, and I regret thinking about fresh air and crashing on the reef. I don't want to die. I don't want to be dragged down into the cold, dark water. I think of all the times I wanted to be a silvery fish. I don't want that any more. I don't want to be in the water. I am not a silvery fish. I won't go flashing and dancing through the water. It will pull me down and smother me in its dark wetness.

There is a shout from above, and Hugh opens the hatch and peers down into the hold. Water pours in after him. It's very dark down here, so I can barely see him.

'Keep praying, children,' he says. 'The storm is bad. We've lost two of the other ships. Make sure you pray hard, and whatever you do, don't leave this hold or you will die.'

I start to tremble. I think of David and Blanchefleur and Alard being choked and smothered by cold, black water. I think of how they would struggle and kick, but the ocean is savage and they are only small. Ines squeezes my hand again and I squeeze back.

Stephan laughs, high and sharp. 'Another test!' he cries. 'Clearly we are not all good and pure. There were still more of us not worthy to serve the Holy Purpose.'

I think about Eustache and what I did. I think about how I doubted Stephan on the beach at Genoa. Am I good and pure? Am I worthy to serve the Holy Purpose? Am I more worthy than David? Or the shivering boy with black fingers? Or little Ami with his cobweb hair?

The ship rolls again and makes a screaming, shuddering noise. We're all thrown on top of each other. The children scream and cry. I cling to Ines and try to hold back tears. I want to be brave.

It rolls and shudders again and this time I hear cracking wood. We're going to die. I hear laughter and I know it is Stephan. Fox-boy scrambles into a crouch.

'Olly-flamb,' he says, breathing hard. 'Broken.'

He twitches and hesitates, and then moves towards the ladder, climbing over the other children.

Lili Wilkinson

'Don't be daft, Fox-boy,' says Ines. 'Leave it.'

Fox-boy turns back and creeps towards her. His fingers brush her cheek.

'Ines,' he says, and then looks at me. 'Fambly.'

'It's just a scrap of cloth. It doesn't *mean* anything,' says Ines, tears rolling down her cheeks.

Fox-boy smiles at her and shakes his head. 'Silly,' he says. 'Silly. Means *evryfing.*'

And he turns and climbs the ladder and disappears into the storm before we can hold him down or stop him. The storm roars down into the hold after him, chasing around the room and whipping us all to the bone.

Ines chokes out a sob.

'Ines,' I shout, over the roar of the water. 'If something happens. If we get separated – I'll find you. I'll find you in the Holy Land.'

'No!' says Ines. 'You won't.'

'I will,' I say. 'We'll fight the Saracen together. We'll rescue Our Lord. We will.'

Ines is shaking with sobs. 'We won't!' she says. 'Don't you see?'

I don't see. I wipe salt water out of my eyes and for a moment I wonder if we are all drowning in an ocean of Stephan's tears.

Ines is white and fierce, though she continues to cry. She looks more alive and awake than she has in days. The vacant look in her eyes is gone, replaced by a look of terror. 'There is no Holy Land!' she screams. 'There *is* no Our Lord. They don't *exist*.'

Her words hit me harder and colder than any ocean wave. For a moment I think I am standing on the edge of a cliff, looking out over black, black nothing as far as the eye can see. It is terrifying and empty.

twenty-six

We don't die. The storm goes away by morning, and as soon as it is safe, Ines and I climb up to the deck and find Fox-boy. He is trapped under a piece of the mast that snapped off and got stuck on the deck. He is all blue and his eyes don't see any more. Clutched tight in one hand is a dirty, ragged scrap of once red fabric, with golden threads trailing from it like tangled hair.

He looks smaller than before. Just a little boy. I don't know how old he was. Younger than me, I think. I remember how much I hated him when he first joined us. But then I named him Fox-boy, and I think after that maybe he belonged to me a little. I touch his cold nose and remember how he snuffled and twitched when he was asleep. I remember him chasing rabbits through the undergrowth and coming back all pink and panting, his face nearly cracking in two for smiling. I wonder if there was a family who missed him. I will miss him.

I prise the remains of the Oriflamme from Fox-boy's hand, and then Ines and I stand over him and say a prayer. I hope I will meet him again in the Holy Land. He was a good friend.

We don't see any of the other ships, and I wonder if I shall ever see Blanchefleur, or Alard, or any of the other children ever again. Maybe they are all dead.

I don't know how many days we spend in the smelly, dark hold, but eventually a sailor shouts out, 'Land!' Then there is a lot of shouting and oars are brought out and the bigger boys help with the rowing.

Stephan is trembling. His breath comes out in little puffs and gasps, and he makes high, squeaking sounds like an animal.

We clamber up out of the hold and onto the deck.

At first it's bright – too bright to see. The sunlight is hot and blinding, and I have to squeeze my eyes closed because it hurts my head. But I open them again, just a crack, until I get used to the light. Then I can look.

The sky and the sea are a beautiful, sparkling blue.

I can see four islands with white buildings close to the mainland, where white walls embrace a city. But it's like no city I've ever seen. The buildings are all white – like they are built from snow. There are no red bricks or thatched roofs or even wooden buildings. Just all white and sparkling.

'Holy,' says Stephan, as tears run down his cheeks. 'Holy. Holy.'

I turn to Ines and grin. 'Look!' I tell her. 'Here we are. The Holy Land.'

Ines bites her lip and frowns but says nothing.

The city rises to a peak where there is a majestic white building with turrets and flags. That must be where Our Lord lives. Beyond the city, I can see green fields and dark forests, and then tall mountains behind them.

But where are the Saracen? And why is the land so green, the buildings so beautiful? I thought that the Saracen had made the plants wither, and the ground barren and burned.

Maybe it is a trick. An illusion. Maybe the Saracen are hiding behind those white walls, ready to attack.

I still don't know how to fight a Saracen.

I take a deep breath. Maybe they are already dead. Perhaps we are close enough now, on this ship, that all the Saracen have fallen down dead because of our purity. And that's why the fields are green again.

We sail past the high white walls into a harbour. There are many ships and boats and barges – too many to count. We are the first of the ships to arrive, but I turn around and can see two more in the distance.

At last, we are here. A gangplank appears from somewhere, and Stephan stumbles down it and throws himself at the stone quay. He presses his forehead against the white stones and weeps and kisses the stone, whispers to it, caresses it.

We follow him down the gangplank and cluster on the white quay, looking around in wonder.

I turn to Ines. 'Now what happens?' I say. 'Where are the Saracen?'

Ines looks past me. 'Something is wrong,' she says.

I follow her gaze and see a group of men coming towards us. They must be priests, because they wear long white robes.

But then I see their skin.

They are black-skinned.

I remember what Stephan said about the black fingers on the mountains, about how it was evil leaking out from inside. Are these men the Saracen?

I thought they would be taller.

There are five of them. Their black skin looks smooth. For a moment I think it is beautiful, then I realise that they must be working a Magic on me. It won't work.

I am strong.

Lili Wilkinson

When they reach Stephan, who is still whispering to the white stones, one of them reaches down and pulls him to his feet.

Stephan takes in their white robes and black skin.

One of the men says something in a tongue that sounds like rocks bouncing and scraping down a hillside. It is the strangest sound I have ever heard, and I can't believe it comes from a person.

If it is a person.

Stephan licks his lips.

'Servants of the Saracen,' he says to the men.

Of course. These black-skinned men are not the Saracen. They are the Saracen's servants. That is why they are normal-sized.

'Servants of the Saracen,' Stephan says again. 'Tremble, for we are the Army of Children.'

'Shut up,' says Ines, suddenly.

Stephan stiffens and glares at her. 'How dare –'

'This isn't it,' she interrupts. 'This isn't the Holy Land. We've been betrayed.'

'No,' says Stephan. 'I can feel it, we are close to Our Lord.'

But I know Ines is right. I feel a familiar bitterness. We turn around and see Hugh the Iron and William the Pig standing behind us. When they see our faces, they start to laugh.

'What have you done?' asks Ines.

They continue to laugh, deep, growling laughs. One of the black-skinned men comes forward and takes Ines's chin in his hand. He says something in his strange tongue. I don't know what it is, but I don't like it.

'Leave her alone,' I say.

The black-skinned man ignores me. He looks down at the silver badges pinned to Ines's dress.

'No,' she whispers. 'Please don't.'

The man grins and rips the badges off Ines, tucking them into a fold of his robe. Then he turns and gives Hugh a red cloth bag that clinks heavily with coins. Hugh hefts the bag, and then turns to return to the ship.

'No!' says Stephan. His face is white and red blotches. 'You can't do this.'

Hugh stops and walks back to Stephan. His sloping eyes don't look sorry any more. He lifts his hand and strikes Stephan across the face, so hard that Stephan drops to the white stones.

'Wicked!' Stephan gasps.

One of the black-skinned men says something sharp to Hugh, who nods and walks up the gangplank onto the ship. William the Pig marches forward and kicks Stephan in the ribs.

twenty-seven

Our clothes are stripped from our backs, and our hands are tied in front of us, and then roped to each other. They take Ines's mortar and pestle, and her little pouch of dried herbs. They take Stephan's wooden cup, which makes him scream and spit. And they take the Oriflamme from my hand.

'No!' I say. 'You mustn't.'

But a dark-skinned man just flashes his white teeth at me. He unfolds the Oriflamme and frowns. It is not very impressive any more. The red is not so much red now as black, and the gold is just shabby brown.

'Let them take it, Gabby,' says Ines. 'It doesn't matter.'

'But Fox-boy –' I say.

'It doesn't matter.'

The dark-skinned man tosses the Oriflamme over the side of the quay into the ocean, and I think that Fox-boy died for nothing.

We are marched naked through the sparkling white city. Stephan has to be carried. He kicks and screams and bites, and white foam comes spilling from his mouth. I think I am more frightened of him than I am of the black men.

I am tied before Ines, but I look over my shoulder and she is right behind me. I want to say something, but it is strange to see her white body with all its unfamiliar parts.

Black-skinned children run through the streets after us, laughing and pointing. Some throw stones.

A woman holding a basket of fruit stops to watch us pass. She is covered from head to toe in thick, black fabric, with only a slit for her eyes. The eyes are large and black and very, very sad. I don't know if she is sad for us, or sad for herself. Maybe both.

The narrow streets open out onto a large paved square full of market stalls. They sell fruits and vegetables I have never seen before, all different colours. Chickens squawk and flap, and goats bleat. Men and women call things out, and the air is so full of yelling and squawking and bleating that for a moment I don't hear the hoarse screaming coming from Stephan. It is just like the market in Briis-sous-Forges, and I remember the feel of Misha's warm breathing underneath my hand, and her brown cow-eyes that knew everything, and her sweet low voice singing up the sun. And I feel myself grow calm.

We are lined up against a wall, and then we wait.

Black-skinned men come and poke us, open our mouths, look at our teeth. They peer into my eyes, examine the soles of my feet, my secret places. They barter and converse with the white-robed men, and then bolts of cloth, glass beads and gold coins are produced, and the larger, stronger boys are led away.

'Ines,' I whisper. 'What is this place?'

She shakes her head. 'I think we are somewhere in Africa,' she says. 'But I am not certain.'

I don't know where Africa is, or if it is close to the Holy Land. I don't know if it matters any more. I wish Fox-boy was here.

'Ines,' I say again. 'We must stay together.'

Ines nods firmly. 'Yes,' she says. 'I won't leave you.'

The sun grows high then begins to sink. I am thirsty.

A man comes to examine us. His skin is lighter than the white-robed men, but it is still very dark. He wears thick, heavy red robes, and a golden chain around his neck with a strange jewel. His hair is grey and black, all mixed in together.

He moves down the line, speaking to each of us. As he nears us, I am surprised to hear that he is speaking our tongue, although it sounds strange.

He stands before Ines. 'Can you read and write?' he says.

Ines nods. 'Yes,' she says. 'The monks taught me.'

The man turns and says something to the white-robed men. One of them comes forward and cuts away the rope that ties me to Ines. I feel like he is cutting my own arm.

'Wait!' I say. 'I can read too.'

The man looks at me and raises his eyebrows.

'I can,' I say. 'I'm very good.'

He reaches into a bag and pulls out a scrap of parchment.

'Read this,' he says. 'Read it to me.'

I look at the parchment. It is covered in little black squiggles and lines. I look at them hard and frown. It can't be that difficult. There must be a trick to it. Maybe if I concentrate hard enough. Maybe if I pray . . .

The man shakes his head and puts the parchment away. Then he counts some coins into the dark man's hand and grabs Ines by the arm.

'No!' I say. 'Wait! I can read! I can!'

'Gabby,' Ines calls, over her shoulder as she is dragged away. 'I'll find you. I promise. Wait for me.'

And then she is gone, swallowed up by chickens and goats and black-skinned men.

We stay in the market until night falls. Most of the children are bought and led away. There are maybe twenty of us left – me, Stephan and the other smallest boys. Then a short man with yellow-brown skin and a curly black beard comes and speaks to the black-skinned men. I hear the clinking of coins, and then the clanking of chains. The chains are placed around our ankles, and we are led out of the city and back to the quay again, where we are pushed onto another ship and covered in darkness.

I wriggle around until I am next to Stephan. He has stopped screaming and kicking, and is lying still.

'Gabriel,' he mutters, his voice all crackling and worn. 'Be strong. Be pure.'

I swallow away tears. I'm trying. I'm trying to be strong. I miss Ines. I miss Fox-boy.

'This is it,' he says. 'This is the final test. We are being taken to the Holy Land. At last.'

I want to believe him. I can't swallow the tears away any more. I cry for my Maman and Papa. I cry for little Orry who ate the wrong sort of mushroom. I cry for Ami, and David, and Luc, and the shivering boy. I cry for Eustache and for Blanchefleur and Alard. I cry for Ines and Fox-boy. But most of all I cry for me.

There are no days or nights on the ship. Just endless rocking and sinking and rising. My sickness returns and I lie with my eyes closed, crammed in with the other children, trying to imagine myself into being a silvery fish.

I imagine shafts of watery light falling on my face. The low-hanging branches *shh, shh, shh* against the water, whispering. I flash and sparkle as my tail flips back and forth. Sometimes, just for fun, I leap out of the water and into the warm, fresh air, droplets of water spinning and flying around me like jewels. Then I plunge back into the smooth, cool water. It folds over me and I sink, sink, sink down to the silty, weedy bottom of the river. My body makes puffs of dust rise on the river floor as it moves through the green leaves that stream upwards like a princess's hair. I flash my tail, making a cloud of brown silt, and push upwards through the water until it is so crystal clear that it's like flying.

But slowly, slowly, the water dries up, until my flashing scales aren't silvery any more. They are dull brown, and my glassy, fishy eye is covered with white cloud. And I sink down into the muddy, silty ground.

I am walking.

I open my eyes. There are yellow rocks underneath my bare feet and all around. My head aches and I feel hot and cold and shivery all at the same time. My mouth is so dry I think maybe it is full of sand.

I don't remember getting off the boat, but I must have because here I am, walking behind Stephan through a rocky, barren wilderness. There are a few scraggly brown tufts of plants, but no green. We are not tied up any more. Maybe we should try to run away. But where would we run to?

'Stephan,' I say, and my voice doesn't work properly, but he hears anyway and looks over his shoulder at me. His eyes are wide with joy and his mouth wrinkles in his secret smile.

'We're nearly there,' he says, 'It's so close.'

Before us are rough, spiky-looking hills. They don't look Holy to me. I don't think I can climb them. I am not strong.

So I fly. I become a sort of fish-bird, with a shimmering body of blue and green scales, and long, white feathered wings. A bird-fish. An Angel fish. I beat my wings and flap and rise and rise until the spiky hills are far below. I look down at the tiny line of boys walking, led by the man with the black beard who rides a black horse.

Where is Stephan? I can't see him in the line. Where is he? Is he safe?

I look around in panic, and then he is there next to me. He is not a bird-fish, he is still a boy. But his arms, stretched out at his sides, narrow into long white feathers that keep him afloat on currents of air. I laugh. Stephan laughs too, and we dive and swoop and twirl through blue air. We don't look at the greyish, broken earth. We don't look at the spiky hills or the crumbling rocks. We just laugh up into the blue, blue sky, blue as an arrow.

It's cold at night, and I wish I had a blanket. I have forgotten how it feels to wear clothes. The ground is hard and lumpy, but we still sleep soundly, we are so tired. I think about the straw mattress I slept on in my house in Machery. I think of how Maman used to lay a sheepskin over it in winter, and how it felt, the first cold night, to snuggle into the soft wool. I think of Papa, getting up before dawn to put more wood on the fire so we would not be cold when we woke.

I miss them. I know I am supposed to be filled with joy to be on this Holy Mission, but I think I want to go home. I wonder where I would be now if I had never gone with Stephan. If I'd never heard his bare feet *shh, shh, shh*-ing along the road to Machery. If I'd never looked into his arrow-blue eyes.

I wouldn't be hungry right now. Or cold. Or naked. Or frightened. I would be safe.

But I never would have met Ines, or Fox-boy.

Or Stephan.

I look over at him. He lies pressed against the rocky ground, his palms facing down, his cheek in the dust as if he is listening to the earth. His eyes are closed, and the secret smile flickers over his lips. He whispers softly to the pebbles and sand.

He is sure this is it. The Holy Land. I am not so sure.

I can't say how many days we have been walking across this strange land. It could be a whole lifetime. But today we stumble over one of the spiky hills and see a city spread out before us.

The sun is high and hot and it lights up the city, all warm and glowing. It is a city of pinkish-white stone, with enormous walls holding it all together. The buildings look strange, curved and arching, more like animals or plants than houses and churches. On the far side I can see a golden dome that shines so brightly, for a moment I think it might be the sun itself. I think of the Oriflamme, a golden sun on a field of red. This place is like that. Golden dome, pink buildings and red, red earth.

Stephan falls to the ground and starts to cry and jabber in words I don't understand.

'Where are we?' I ask. 'What is this?'

The man with the black beard turns on his horse and looks down at me. I hope he will not beat me.

'Don't you know?' He says. I didn't know he could speak our tongue. 'This is the Holy City.'

twenty-eight

Everything is different.

The pinkish animal buildings are so unlike the wooden houses at home. They are smooth and somehow graceful. There are strange towers everywhere, tall and slender, with onion-shaped domes on top.

Everyone dresses in loose cotton robes. The men wear white, the women, black. The women all have their heads covered. Some cover their faces too, like the women in the African city. Except these women are not black-skinned. Their skin is browner than mine, but it is not the kind of brown that you get when evil is leaking out of you. It is a sun-brown, like thick, dark honey.

The men wear white scarves on their heads, all twisted round and round. I think that if I wore such long skirts I would trip over, but nobody does. There are golden bands on their sleeves, embroidered with black squiggles that might be their writing. Everybody wears open leather sandals.

Stephan hisses and twists against his chains and ropes. 'Saracen,' he spits. 'Saracen!'

I look around. I can't see any Saracen. Just men and women. They talk to each other in low voices. Their tongue is the strangest I have heard yet, with vibrating *mmms* and full, throaty sounds.

Stephan stops, so I walk into him.

'Careful, Gabriel,' he says. 'This is it. This is when we will fight the Saracen.'

I look around. A veiled woman leads a little girl down the street by the hand. The girl is chattering at her mother. I frown.

'Careful of their horns,' says Stephan. 'Careful of their sharp hoofs. And remember that their breath is as hot as fire.'

We walk past an open paved area. There is a domed building in the middle – not the big golden dome I saw from the hill, but a smaller version. There is a trough of water outside, and lines and lines of empty shoes.

At first I think it is a shop, but then I see a man come

up, remove his shoes, and wash his hands and feet in the trough. Then he pads inside the domed building and I realise it is a kind of church.

'Don't be frightened,' says Stephan. 'I know they look terrible, but we are strong. We are pure.'

We are brought to another marketplace, much like the one in Africa. There is a white-robed man there waiting for us. His face looks sour and bored. Our keeper speaks to him in the strange throaty tongue. The man frowns and replies, his voice harsh and full of spite.

I look up and around. I can see a glint of gold behind the strange onion towers. The golden dome, beautiful and shining like the Oriflamme.

Stephan is panting. His face is pink and shining with sweat. He needs help. We both need help.

We need Our Lord.

And I know where to find him.

Our keeper and the white-robed man begin to yell at each other, stabbing their hands at the air. They are not looking at us. Now is the time.

I grab Stephan's elbow. 'Come on!' I say. 'Run!'

Stephan just stands there as I tug, and I think I might pull him over into the dirt, but finally his legs start moving and I half-drag him off through the square.

There is a shout from behind us, but I don't look back. Stephan finally realises what's happening, and takes off as fast as a rabbit, his long legs lifting high and his secret parts swinging and bouncing against his thighs.

We do not go unnoticed – two naked boys, pink and peeling from the sun, racing through the market, upsetting baskets of grains and strange-looking fruits. People shout and try to grab us, and a little boy points and laughs so hard he falls over.

But we duck and we scramble until we are out of the market square and sprinting down a narrow street, lined with pink-stone buildings. I look up to see where the golden dome is, and spot it glinting off in the distance. I swerve down a different street towards it.

The shouts from the market have died down, but we do not slow. Our Lord is waiting. Stephan starts to laugh, high and panting and scratchy.

'Yes,' he says. 'Yes. It is time.'

I don't know what it is time for, but I don't care any more. I am done listening to Stephan. It's time to find Our Lord and finish this.

A dog runs out in front of us in the street. It is thin with a wiry grey coat. I try to stop but it gets all tangled up in my legs and I fall over on my face in the orange dirt.

Stephan trips over me and we all end up in a heap, me and the dog and Stephan, all arms and legs and paws and wiry grey fur. Stephan's breathing is shallow and his pupils are enormous. He takes little gasping half-breaths, his mouth open wide. Dirt and tiny stones are burning a long scrape up my knees and wrists. I spit out dirt. The dog licks my face, and I push it away. It smells like dog, and I think of Fox-boy and I think maybe some of the dirt got into my throat because I can't swallow.

'Come on,' I say to Stephan. 'We're nearly there.'

I pull him to his feet. I think I twisted my ankle when I fell, but I ignore it and we run on.

We run up a flight of steps and through a series of stone arches and come out into the open.

The sun is low, staining the pink buildings a deep, velvety red. The sun wraps around the golden dome and it shines and gleams red and gold and orange like it is alive. It is like the Oriflamme come to life, a burning, living sun, surrounded by red and shadow. There is a curved golden moon on top of the dome, and I think that maybe having the sun and the moon there together in the sky is the biggest miracle I've seen yet.

We run inside.

'Yes!' cries Stephan. 'He is here! I can feel him!'

It is like being inside the sun. Above us the dome shines with warm gold reflections of flickering torches. Painted flowers in red and gold twist and creep up the pillars and columns like they are trying to reach the sky.

A great rock lies under the dome. It looks strange, all twisted and raw against the perfect lines and swirls of gold and marble.

Stephan runs forward, and I hear his feet go *slap,*

slap, slap on the cold, smooth floor. He turns around and looks up, holding his arms out. I can hear his breathing, fast and rough.

'I am here,' says Stephan. 'I have come.'

I look around for Our Lord, but I don't see Him. Instead I see a dark man whose face is red with fury.

He is very large, with a sword strapped to his back. He looks like he just ate something that turned out to be rotten inside, his mouth twisted in disgust.

He speaks in the strange throaty tongue at us, and although I don't understand it, I know he is furious. I think he is going to kill us with his hands. He reaches out and hesitates for a moment, like touching our nakedness will make him sick. Then he wraps one enormous arm around my waist and picks me up. He wraps the other arm around Stephan, who wriggles and kicks and screams. The man drops him to the floor and grabs him by one ankle, and drags us out of the great domed building.

Outside, the sun has sunk below the hills, and the pink buildings are now purple, swallowed up in shadows. The dome isn't on fire any more, and the gold is dull without the sunlight.

Torches are being lit, breathing smoke and sparks up into the deep purple sky.

The man throws me down onto the stones that are still warm from the sun, and lets forth a blazing stream of hatred in his tongue.

Stephan has grown silent and still. He pushes himself up. He is covered in dirt and peeling skin and grazes. His eyes are shining and wet.

'Saracen,' he says, his voice utterly calm. 'We are pure and true and Holy. It is time for you to leave this place.'

The man draws the enormous, curved sword from his back.

I hear footsteps running in the distance, getting closer. The man narrows his eyes. Stephan stands up until he is almost face-to-face with the man.

He smiles his secret smile. 'You cannot kill me,' he says. 'I am the leader of the Children's Army, and I will have victory over the Holy Land.'

And I believe him.

Right there, among the shadowy purple buildings with their onion-towers and their strange men and women in their black and white robes, I believe him. All my doubts have gone. My misery, my bitterness. It doesn't matter that the Saracen aren't seven feet tall. It doesn't matter that Eustache and Fox-boy and Blanchefleur are dead, and probably Ines too. It doesn't matter that the ocean didn't part at Genoa.

Stephan is Holy. He is pure. And we will have victory.

I hear the footsteps come closer, hear them going *shh, shh, shh* on the ground, and I remember the first time Stephan's eyes arrowed into mine. I remember the stick that he used to draw the alpha fish in the dirt.

I am the alpha fish. And Stephan is my King.

Then the Saracen's sword comes down on Stephan's neck.

twenty-nine

There is blood everywhere. It runs down over Stephan's crumpled body and washes my feet, warm and thick, before it seeks the cracks between the stones and sinks into the ground.

I cannot move.

Stephan's eyes are open, but they aren't arrow-blue any more. They are dark and empty. His mouth has lost its secret smile.

The Saracen turns to me. Blood drips from the sword. He raises it again and I close my eyes and wonder if

Ines was right about Our Lord. I'll find out soon.

I hear a shout from behind me, and the Saracen's sword freezes as he turns.

A man's voice speaks, but I do not turn to see it. I can't see anything except the limp arms and legs that used to be Stephan. I can't feel his tears burning inside me any more. I can't feel anything.

The Saracen with the sword says something curt. The person behind me responds in a calm voice, speaking quickly and firmly. The Saracen lowers his sword.

I feel a hand on my shoulder.

'Are you all right, boy?' says a voice. It speaks my tongue carefully, like the words are the wrong size.

I feel myself being gently turned around, and I look up and see a face.

It is a bearded face, round and red-cheeked. Kind brown eyes are sloped down under concerned brows. The hair is tight and dark and curled. I swallow.

The man who saved me from the Saracen is round and tall. He looks strong and wise. He looks like the kind of man who would like singing and honey-cakes.

'Come,' he says. 'Let us go to my home.'

I start to follow him without thinking, then I turn to look at the body crumpled on the pale stone. The Saracen with the sword bows down to the ground and scoops up the body like it is not heavy at all. Then he walks away with it.

The last I ever see of Stephan is an ankle, swinging free against the Saracen's hip, and a dark stain on white stone.

The bearded man lives in a pink stone house not very far from the golden dome. Inside it is cool and clean. A red and blue carpet lies on the floor, with a twisting pattern that makes me think of flowers. Low benches with bright fabrics line the walls, and there is a little table covered in paper and many leather-bound books.

The man picks up one of the pieces of cloth from a bench and hands it to me.

'Here,' he says. 'Cover yourself.'

I take it. My cheeks burn as I wrap the cloth around me. It is soft and beautifully patterned in strange green and red shapes. It smells strange, like spices I have never tasted. I wonder if this is silk.

The man sits down on one of the low benches and indicates that I do the same.

He opens a small wooden box containing some small, shiny brown lumps. They look like a cross between cockroaches and cow pats. He holds the box out to me.

'Here,' he says. 'Take one.'

I do, but then I'm not sure what to do with it. The man also takes a brown thing, and pops it into his mouth. I'm supposed to eat it?

'It's a date,' says the man. 'You will like it.'

I am not so sure. I nibble at the brown thing. The shininess is just a very thin shell, and underneath it is creamy and sweet. I shove the whole thing in my mouth and chew. It tastes like honey-cakes and the warm sleepy darkness just before dawn.

The man watches me eat the date. There is a stone at the heart of it, but I do not spit it out. I suck and chew on it, getting every last bit of sweetness. It has been a long time since I ate a proper meal.

'My name is Mujir ibn al-Nafis. I am a scholar.'

'Gabriel,' I tell him. 'My name is Gabriel.'

He smiles. 'Like the Angel,' he says. 'We have this Angel too, except here we say Jibreel. He has six hundred wings, and is the bearer of our most sacred text.'

Six hundred wings sounds strange to me. But this man seems to know about Angels, which makes me almost certain I know who he is.

I take a deep breath. 'Are you Our Lord?' I ask, my voice all high like a girl's.

The bearded man blinks and stares at me for a moment. Then he starts to laugh, a deep belly-laugh that rumbles and echoes around the room.

'No, Jibreel,' he says. 'I am not. I am just a man.'

I sigh. 'Then do you know where he is? Our Lord?'

The man chuckles. 'It is a question that men have been asking since the beginning of time.'

He offers me another date and I take it.

'I'm sorry,' I say, my mouth full of creamy brown. 'But if you are not Our Lord, then does that mean you are a Saracen?'

'That is what your people would call me.'

I am confused. 'But you don't look like a Saracen.'

'Really?' says the man. 'What did you think a Saracen would look like?'

'Tall,' I say. 'And wicked and evil with horns and smoke coming out your nose.'

The man laughs again. 'You must be very disappointed.'

'But you are invaders,' I say. 'Monsters!'

The man sighs. 'My little friend,' he says. 'In this city, it is *you* who are the invader.'

'But the Saracen took over the Holy City,' I say. 'You stole it from us.'

'Yes,' he says. 'But before that, you stole it from us.'

'But who had it first?' I say.

The man folds his hands. 'Neither of us,' he says. 'First it belonged to the Judeans.'

I shake my head. I have never heard of a Judean. 'What is a Judean?' I ask. 'Is it a monster? Like a Saracen?'

'A Judean is a man,' says the man. 'We are all men, and sometimes we are all monsters.'

I blink. 'But I'm not a monster,' I say. 'I don't want to punish Our Lord.'

'Neither do I,' says the man. 'Neither do any of us.

My Lord is different to your Lord. And to the Lord of the Judeans. That is all.'

I don't understand any of this. 'There's more than one?'

'I do not know. There are things that men are not supposed to know.'

I wonder if Stephan knew. I wonder if he knew anything at all. I think about Maman and Papa and our house in Machery. I remember Misha the cow, and the way she sang the sun up. I remember Ines and Fox-boy.

'I want to go home,' I say.

The man purses his lips, head on one side.

'Jibreel,' he says at last, 'I cannot let you go. You are an escaped slave, and if you are caught you will be executed. If you try to leave the Holy City, you will perish in the mountains.'

I nod. So this is it, then. I shall die after all.

'There are people of your kind in this city though. There is a church, with priests. I could take you to them to live.'

I close my eyes and see the paintings and carvings of Our Lord in the abbey at St Denis. I see His sad eyes. And then I see Stephan's eyes, dead and empty and not arrowing into anything any more.

'No,' I say. 'I have had enough of Our Lord, whoever and wherever He is.'

The man pops another date into his mouth and chews

thoughtfully. 'Well,' he says. 'I could try to purchase you.
You could stay here and work for me.'

I look up at him, at his dark beard and shiny cheeks.
I don't know what I want.

thirty

'Jibreel,' calls my master.

He is a good master. He is kind and patient, and has taught me to speak his tongue. He has even taught me all the Greek letters that come after alpha. We have been together now for nine years.

I keep his house tidy, and bring him dates with milk and honey when he is hungry. In the evenings, we walk through the streets of the Holy City, and then sit in the shade of the great golden dome and we eat a banana each.

'Eating a banana,' says my master, 'in the shadow of the dome, is one of the things that makes life wonderful.'

I agree. I like bananas. They are sweet and smooth and delicious. I like all of the food here in the Holy City, but bananas and dates are my favourites. There is no cabbage.

The day after I met my master, he brought me back to the golden dome, to the place where the end of Stephan's life still stained the white stone. And he told me everything.

'One hundred years ago,' he said, 'the city was ours. Your soldiers came in and murdered people – men, women, children. The stories say that the streets ran with rivers of blood, up to your knees.'

I wanted to tell him that I didn't believe him. But I said nothing.

'The soldiers did not bury the dead,' said my master. 'They just left them to rot, and then, three days after they arrived, they held a market to sell each other the treasures they had ripped from the corpses. Five months later, there were still bodies lying in the streets.'

I remembered the Holy soldiers in the heathen village. I remembered how horrified Ines was when Fox-boy chewed on a bone.

I know the whole story now. About how after nearly one hundred years, my master's people took back the Holy City. But this time there was no massacre. Not one person was killed. The nobles were allowed to buy their freedom, and everyone else was to be sold as slaves. But the Saracen King realised that families would be separated, and let many of them go. The King's brother asked for a thousand slaves and released them all immediately.

I wept when I first heard that story. I weep again now, as I remember it.

My master has invited me to pray with him. I am honoured – it's a sign of great respect. People pray a lot here. Five times a day, men climb the tall onion-towers – minarets – and call out to all the people to go and pray. And everybody drops what they're doing and goes to the nearest temple, removes their shoes and washes their hands and feet, and prays.

I ask my master what happens if they can't get to a temple.

'Then they pray wherever they are,' he tells me. 'As long as they face towards the Holy City.'

It is sort of funny, that the people who live in our Holy City have a Holy City of their own, far to the south.

'I can teach you the prayers,' says my master. 'If you wish.'

I thank him, but refuse.

'Then,' he says, 'would you prefer to travel to the other side of the city and pray with your own kind?'

Again, I refuse. I don't pray any more. Nothing good seems to come of it.

I like the look of Holy buildings. The temples are round and soft, as if they are embracing the earth beneath them.

There is a church here too. It looks like it is pushing up into the sky, trying to fly like a white bird. I know it will be cool and quiet and calm inside.

But I never go in.

I don't want to see the statues of Our Lord, or the paintings. I don't want to see His sad, sad eyes. Because now, finally, I understand why He is so sad.

My master sends me out in the afternoon to the market to buy lamb and bread for our dinner. As I am leaving, a messenger comes in to speak to my master. He says that there is a noblewoman from the west who wishes to see him. I am about to ask my master what the woman wants, but I can't find my other sandal, so I forget.

The market is clean and orderly. Pine nuts, dates and raisins fill wicker baskets, and large barrels are filled with thick golden honey. The merchants here all know me, and we nod and I practise talking in my awkward version of their tongue. They are patient, and smile with flashing white teeth, and answer with slow, clear words.

'Jibreel,' says Nasim, who sells dates and raisins and pine nuts. '*As-Salamu alaikum.*'

Lili Wilkinson

I like this greeting. It means 'peace be unto you', which is the nicest thing you can wish someone.

'*Wa alaikum assalam*,' I reply, and give a little bow, which makes Nasim smile, although he might have been smiling because I said something wrong.

'Have you prayed today, Jibreel?' Nasim asks. He asks this every time we meet.

'No, Nasim,' I reply.

Nasim shakes his head and looks very sad. But I know he is not all serious. We do this nearly every day, and I think he finds me funny. The pale-skinned *kafir* who doesn't pray. *Kafir* is their word that means to them what Saracen means to us. Although my master tells me that I am not really a *kafir*. I am a Person of the Book. I had never really seen a book before I came here, so he might be wrong. But he says that a Person of the Book is a person who has an Our Lord, even if it is not the same one as their Our Lord. It's all very confusing, and sometimes I think maybe I am a *kafir* after all.

I buy a handful of pine nuts, and move on to the other stalls.

I buy spiced ground lamb and bread, and also some soft white cheese, and some ripe yellow quinces.

I remember the wriggly old quince trees at St Denis, and the dirt under Ines's fingernails. I remember the day, very early on, when Ines asked me what I thought the Holy Land would look like.

'It is beautiful,' I told her. 'It is all soft grass and fruit trees and clear streams full of apple cider and silvery fish.'

I was wrong. It is nothing like that. Nothing at all like I imagined. But it is still beautiful. More beautiful, perhaps, because it is a real place and not a dream place.

The streams *are* clear, and sometimes I see the flick and shiver of a silvery fish disturbing the silt at the bottom. But the banks of the streams are not lined with soft green grass. Instead they are fringed with long, spiky cattails that cut you when you try to push through them. And instead of forests of trees heavy with apples and apricots, there are long, straight groves full of silvery-green olive trees, all twisted in and around like stooped old men.

I still look up at the stars, sometimes, and wonder if they really are a glimpse through the cracks into some kind of Holy Land.

My master laughed when I told him that. He says that stars are thousands of lights, very far away in the sky, like tiny suns. The first time I heard that, I was very frightened. I remembered being on the ship in that storm with Ines, the terror in her eyes as she screamed at me. I remembered feeling like I was on the edge of a cliff, looking out over a whole world of empty black nothing, going on forever.

But now I am not frightened any more. I like the idea of there being thousands of tiny suns, so that no matter how far you fell into the sky, there'd always be one to light your way.

I think Ines would have liked the thousands of tiny suns too.

'Gabby,' says her voice in my mind, and I smile. I wonder where she is now. I hope she is happy.

'Gabby,' says the voice again, louder this time, and I realise it isn't inside my head at all, but behind me.

I turn around, and Ines is there.

thirty-one

She is beautiful.

She's wearing a long, dark dress, blue with twisted lines of silver. Her hair is warm and shining and wound up over her ears. A jewelled necklace hangs around her neck, and there are rings on her fingers.

She looks softer. Her cheeks are fuller and pink. Her lips are dark and her eyes are large and full of tears.

'Gabby,' she says again, her voice deep and sad and throaty, and then moves forward and throws her arms around me. She smells of roses and rain and sunshine.

I take her to the low wall where my master and I sit in the evenings. I buy her a banana and watch her face as she eats it.

She tells me about how she was taken to Egypt, and worked there as a translator for the Pharaoh for five years. Then Pietr arrived, a merchant from the north.

'He was so kind to me,' she says. 'So attentive.'

Pietr took her home with him, and they were married.

'I have a son,' she says. 'He's three years old.'

She puts her banana skin down carefully. 'When I heard Pietr was coming to the Holy City,' she says, 'I came too. Just to see if it really existed.' She laughs. 'He didn't want to let me come. He said it wasn't right for a woman. But he knows not to get in between me and the thing I want.'

I remember when Ines told me she was joining the Children's Army, and smile.

'It does exist,' I tell her. 'The Holy City.'

'I can see that.'

I look around at the cool shadows and hot stones. 'But it isn't what I thought it would be. It's not like we were told.'

'No,' says Ines. 'But it's still beautiful.'

I nod, pleased she sees it too. We sit there for a while, watching the people pass by.

'How did you know where to find me?' I say at last.

'I asked,' she replies. 'I ask wherever I go, every time

I visit a new city, just in case. Someone mentioned a pale slave who refuses to pray.'

I tell her about Stephan. It is a sad story to tell. I don't think of him very often any more, although I always look for a stain on the pale stones where he was killed. There is none any more. No mark of him.

She tells me that Niklaus is alive. She has heard that Pope Innocent refused to help him, and now he is a hermit living somewhere in the hills around Rome.

'Have you seen him?' I ask, and her eyes turn sad.

She shakes her head. 'No,' she says. 'I don't want to.'

Then she looks directly at me. 'I've spoken to your master,' she says. 'He has agreed to let you go free, although he says he will miss you.'

I look back at her, confused.

Ines takes my hand. 'I've come to take you home.'

Home. I think about Machery, and Maman and Papa. I think of the stream and the other boys in the village – who would all be men, now. I think of the little stone church and Father Sebastian. I think of our tiny wooden hut with two rooms. I think of the cow shed. It all seems so small.

Ines has a bright, smiling face. She is expecting me to throw my arms around her and thank her. So why am I not doing that?

'Gabriel? You do want to go home, don't you?'

It is strange to hear my name said that way again.

I am so used to being Jibreel. The sun is setting, sinking down into the west. Home is that way. All I have to do is follow the sun, let it pull me down with it, back to Machery.

Sunset is the best time to be in the Holy City. The buildings all light up and glow pink and orange. Behind us, the great golden dome flares and blushes a deep, rosy gold. The stone wall we are sitting on is warm and smooth, holding in the heat of the day.

From the top of the minaret towers, I hear men singing out, calling the people to pray. Their tongue doesn't sound so strange any more.

'Home,' I say, trying it out.

And I realise that I *am* home. This is my city with its golden dome and bananas and warm, pink stone. Even though I am a slave. Even though I am the invader, the monster. This is my home.

I remember the blackness. The edge of the cliff. I look up and see one or two stars appearing in the purple sky, as soft and deep as velvet.

Ines squeezes my hand. She has tears in her eyes.

I'm standing on the cliff again. I'm still all alone, and the blackness looks very deep, and very dark. But now I realise it is full of stars. This time I'm not scared.

This time I have wings.

Author's note and acknowledgements

History is a strange thing.

The story of the Children's Crusade has been chronicled in many places, and there are many different versions – the story of the German boy Nicholas was even the inspiration for the story of the Pied Piper of Hamelin. But sometimes it is hard to separate the stories from the facts.

There are almost no contemporary records of the Children's Crusade, and the records that do exist are vague and contradictory. There were certainly two expeditions of some kind, one originating in northern France, the other in the Rhineland (modern Germany). Records state that these marches were carried out by *pueri*, which has been translated as 'children'. But it is unlikely they were all children. A chronicler in Cologne wrote years later that the Army 'ranged in age from six years to full maturity'. Other records said that they were teenagers, others that they were elderly people. The only thing that is clear is that these armies were made up of people who were traditionally powerless: peasants, farmers, young people and unmarried women.

It appears that there were two leaders called Nicholas and Stephan, and they led their armies through the same areas at around the same time, although it is not clear if they ever met.

History books will tell you the story of the Children's Crusade much as I have told it here – the journey across the Alps, the failure at Genoa, the betrayal by William the Iron and Hugh the Pig, and eventual slavery. It is not clear what happened to the armies after this point, although it is thought that some of the participants ended up as slaves in Jerusalem.

But how much of that story is truth? What really happened? It is impossible to say. This is both the curse and the wonder of history. All we can do is ask questions and tell stories, and I have tried to do both with this book.

Thanks to my first readers – Sarah Dollard and Carole Wilkinson – for your excellent, encouraging and honest feedback.

The following books were invaluable resources for information and inspiration:

Armstrong, Karen, 1996, *A History of Jerusalem*, Harper Perennial.
Beitzel, Barry J, 2007, *Biblica: The Bible Atlas*, Viking.
Runciman, Steven, 1951, *A History of the Crusades,* Vol. III, Cambridge.
Tyerman, Christopher, 2006, *God's War: A New History of the Crusades*, Penguin.

Thanks also to everyone at black dog who worked on this book.

About the author

Lili Wilkinson remembers the day in Beijing when she learnt to read 'in her head'. She was six and has been immersed in the world of books since. It's an obsession she shares with her mother, author Carole Wilkinson. Lili was first published when she was only eleven in *Voiceworks*, a creative writing magazine for young people. Following an honours degree in Creative Arts and six months of teaching English in Japan, Lili began working at the Centre for Youth Literature, State Library of Victoria. Lili lives in inner Melbourne, and loves reading, quality TV, the work of Jim Henson and Japanese food.

Her first novel SCATTERHEART is also published by Catnip.

To find out more about Lili Wilkinson and Catnip books, go to:

www.catnippublishing.co.uk